Oiseau

The King Catcher

Jesse Byrd

OISEAU THE KING CATCHER

Oiseau The King Catcher

Library of Congress Card Catalog Number: TXu001938350

ISBN: 978-0-578-16804-3

eISBN:

10 9 8 7 6 5 4 3 2 1

Printed in the United States of America

Acknowledgments

To the mother who believed. The father who instilled. The brother who supported. The family who inspired. The friends who light the fire and the love of my life.

"...hidden treasures, riches stored in secret places..."

Chapter 1

"Where there is division, there is strife. You separate one group from another and calamity follows. It may start as appreciation, admiring their differences, but when disagreement pushes and patience sheds its fur, those differences are dangerous. They become lines in the sand," Pierre's father swept his focus across the small cave.

Pierre harbored curiosity about the war, its genesis, persistence, but was too timid to pose the pointed questions. This time, since his father brought it up, now was as good of time as any. "What started all of this? I mean, how do penguins get here?"

"Before my time. I was dropped into it just like you and just like you I'm sure with a lot of the same questions. Some of our answers were lost in history, forcing us to create our own. Some are hidden in our legends and stories, leaving out parts that make us share the blame. No one alive today is sure who struck first. Everyone's a victim."

Pierre scrunched his brows munching his first fish. He loved when his mom picked Mackerel. Mackerel was his absolute favorite. Just saying the word took him to a place. But even dinner that night couldn't pull him from the conversation.

"Why do it?" Pierre said through stuffed cheeks. "If we don't remember why we're fighting," he shrugged, "why do we? Why do they?"

"It doesn't matter. The old 'why' is irrelevant, new ones are born every day. The starting point is subjective for this war, but the loss is not, and neither the potential of losing more. That's what drives us to sharpen beaks and spike our talons. Protection. You live here long enough, and it chews you whole. A sickness, whispering: them or us? Them or us? Them or us? Who will die? Starts to feel like a necessity."

Pierre's cold wet body became warm with unease. He frowned at the sand. "This isn't a necessity."

"Death is."

"Murder isn't."

His father crooked his neck. "Depends on who you ask. What you don't understand is a lot of the waddlers were brought up providing for their troops. Troops of fathers, uncles and cousins. You think they'll let that go? If someone killed us, would you? You would blame them, for doing what they had to do, to see their family come home? Everyone deserves to be coddled, Pierre. No matter where they were hatched. In your limited vision you never had to wrestle with these things. You grew up in a more peaceful time; the young weren't required to serve. Your mother and I did not."

Pierre was quiet. His father never talked about killing. Not even alluded to it in his home. In this cave, he said, he wanted there to be peace, even if this was the only place it was. Pierre loosened his beak.

"Have some Mackerel," his brother suggested, plopping the largest one of the bunch at his webbed feet.

He almost forgot Craig was there. A strong, erect portrait of black and white sitting tall, blotted with healed and healing scars across his chest neck and flippers. Pierre tightened his brow. Why is he serving me fish? "Thanks," he stared at his brother, gobbling it whole.

Pierre shook his head. "That's no excuse," he pressed, talking once again through gaps in consumption.

"You can't...just...take a life...'cause you're scared. Fear," he swallowed and sat straight like a noble, "shouldn't be...the only reason...we fight."

His father leaned forward. "Pierre, we fight for many reasons. Some for love, some for hate, some for pride, some for safety, some for fear and some for a future. But whatever drives us to the field, we all end up there. Every one of us. There is no escape."

His brother shuffled, "That's why it's worse than ever." Pierre squinted as he worked on his last fish. "Why now?"

His father slouched with a glassed gaze. "Because pressure must alleviate itself."

At that moment, Pierre twisted as the pale illumination from outside went away. A figure stepped into the arched portal of their small cave, lingering in the glow, watching them before she entered.

"And we do not want you around for the alleviation," his mom's words were soft and soothing. She gave his father a nod, and found a soft spot across from her mate.

This was getting weird. Thoughts bounced about Pierre's mind, processing the words. They were speaking in code. Talking around and over instead of to and at.

"What do you mean?"

His father and mother were silent in the open space, then his dad moved behind his mom, touching her with his flippers at both sides. "We sent word by albatross to our family in Sud Afrique. You'll have to go tonight."

"We want you to stay with Patricia and Ferdinand for a while."

"We'll send word to let you know when it's safe to come home."

Pierre's jaw tightened. Fury washed over him like hot water as he erupted from his place. "What? You're sending me away? No. No!" He shook his head. "Why do I have to go? Why can't you come with me? I don't want to leave you here if it's getting worse! Are you crazy! I don't care about this place. We can go!"

His mother blinked round tired eyes. "At our age, sweetie, we'd never survive the trip."

"Plus, we are already too many birds short," his father stepped in, "The East needs us."

"And they need me. As a Catcher. So it's settled."

His dad pursed his beak. "Your brother and cousins have agreed on rotating double days. To cover your shifts until we find a replacement."

His mother pushed a few more fish from the middle into his space. "It shouldn't be hard to make up your share. Now please, eat, you'll need your strength."

"I'm the only one." Pierre stared at his brother. "I'm the only one?"

His mother reached for his cheek. He pulled away. "You're it. The only one young enough to have a new beginning, but old enough to survive the trip. You haven't seen what we have. There's no hate in your heart. You have to leave while you're pure, while you can still think good of others, before it won't let you."

His brother looked down at the three small fish in front of him. "I know you don't understand little brother, and in a sense, we don't want you to."

"As your dad, I wanted to keep you ignorant, but especially now you deserve to know what's going on. The war is no longer civil. The West is poisoning rations. Three reserves to be sure. We don't know how or—"

"There's no poison on the Falklands," Pierre snapped, a crack in his voice, knowing he was out of line. Normally he would've been heavily scolded. His father ignored it.

Craig poked his meal. "One of the medics said he'd seen the plants we found in our supply on the big land. They're closer to the land, they can get to things we can't."

Pierre's beak moved slightly, nothing came out. Regardless of what they explained, it worked to only anger him in different ways.

"Little ones are sick!" his mother yipped and the words startled him.

Craig swung down with his right wing, exploding small bits into the air. "They don't deserve to live!"

His brother's muscles tensed. "What kind of..." Craig sniffed violently, "can poison a fledgling!"

His mother jolted. A tear shot down her face. "Nothing is too much."

His father stepped squarely in front of him. "We have to get you out of here. You will have a future, Pierre. Look at me. A real future. Where you can walk with your young without the threat of an ambush. Or swim with your mate and not fear who might be lurking."

He stooped, searching Pierre's face. "Don't rob us. Of knowing the fruit of your eggs will grow in peace. That they, they can do belly flops and nosedives instead of jousts and thrusts. We have to know you are in a better place."

His mother's trembling cheeks pressed two watery streaks. "Please?"

"Let us have it son." His father moved and wrapped himself around her, and for a breath, everything was still.

Errraaacccckkkk!

A stampede of angry squawks charged through the night. The four peered westward at the cave wall, imagining what was to come.

His brother grumbled, then panned from father to mother to brother. "Pierre."

"Craig."

They nodded. Craig ducked out of the cave.

His father wiped his mother's face, then his own. "It's time. We've done a lot for this distraction." His parents rushed him out to shore. "Make sure you're not followed."

"It's only for a while sweetie, then we can be together."

His father walked into the crashing waves. "Listen. Head straight that way." He pointed into the dark horizon. "Past the Georgias, and the South Sandwiches. You should reach Bouvet in half a day's time."

"Rest there two days. Gather your strength, then head north for Sud Afrique. Your aunt and uncle will be at the southern shore sun-fall of the third day."

His mother gasped. "Never forget we love you very much. Now go, while the tide is low."

"See you soon, son. Take care of your aunt and uncle."

His father hugged him long and tight as his mother rested her head on his shoulder. His father pulled her softly away. The loud noise was close.

His father looked into the shadows "You have to go." Urgency filled his eyes, strong and pleading.

Pierre turned, and trod toward the ocean, until it finally pulled him in.

Chapter 2

Splashing water trailed Pierre as he seeped from visibility. His heart pumped manically, his thoughts puffed with frustration and hurt before taking a steady drop into fear.

The ocean below looked like a vapid cave, motionless and void of life. But Pierre knew this was not true. There was life down there. Of the very worst kind.

The grim South Atlantic concealed the secrets of the deep and Pierre could see no further than a hundred yards down.

The liquid sloshed as he kept a covert pace. Fast enough not to be static but slow enough not to draw company. His focus darted, straining to see what he hoped he wouldn't.

After hours of reacting to every sound with wide eyes and stiff movement, Pierre's rigor grew fatigued. 'Somethings' that constantly turned to nothings made him think his imaginations of what was in the dark were more significant than whatever could be. Sharks, tigers, bears...barracudas! Bears riding sharks! Tigers chucking barracudas! His delusions threatened to pull him under until he escaped to the upper world. Pierre spent the first stint of this trip nervously looking down so he chose to spend the next stretch looking up.

Water spilled down the side of his face as he was greeted by numerous faint twinkles in the sky. Seeing what he thought were friends out here reminded him that not everything is scary. Sometimes it's what you choose to look at. The stars off the coast of his homeland were brilliant and he spent every clear summer night directly beneath them. His lax smile was weak and weary. Formerly clamped stubborn muscles waned and unclenched. Awe spread from his chest, warm, relaxing. "They have to be more than what I think they are," he said. They had this magic, a dance-chant, a sparkling séance. He couldn't make sense of it, he didn't fully speak their language but couldn't stop staring. He sailed on his back lost in thought. He needed this friendship, this relationship, whatever it is. Impulses petitioned him to be vigilant, but the sky was tranquil and alluring, making other thoughts a small shout in the distance.

"We have a bond," Pierre thought, stars and penguins, he was sure. A history told in blinking code like they knew each other in a time past. His sleep kept recurring dreams sometimes where the sky was the ocean and the ocean was the sky and he would swim through the air, weaving constellations in an endless collection of white. His eyes closed with hopes to dock at that world, while a steady stroke pushed him forward. The cool water lapped his back and the waves that once roared like woken behemoths were now a soft symphony for serenity. The wind tickled his back. He scrunched. It tickled again. He squirmed, laughed. It tickled a third.

Slowly, his lids came open. His cheeks fell. A thump climbed in his ribcage as his mind met a simple fact. How could the wind tickle his back, if his back was in the water? If not the wind... Pierre took in a breath and slowly churned toward the ocean. Facing the murky abyss, to his surprise, nothing changed. He couldn't see a thing. The darkness wouldn't betray its children. If something were down there, it would be lovingly cloaked.

It reminded him of academy when every Catcher was required to complete exercises in predatory tactics and evasion. The courses were droll and long as time drug through mud to monotonous elocution. He abhorred every bit. Yet, in this moment Pierre struggled to recall something, anything that might now be of help. Particles of a memory crawled, labored, clawed to come forth. A voice was drifting. Clear. Warped. Further. Closer.

"A penguin's greatest advantage is his or her sight," said the professor with the large eyes. Smoke clearing in Pierre's memory dropped him at the scene. "It's why we hunt when the sun is at its highest point. The brightest time of day." He remembered the rasp in his instructor's voice and how misleading it was. His teacher only talked while teaching. Outside of that he communicated solely in frowns, nods, and shrugs. Why was he so hoarse?

"Seeing our prey is what makes us effective. And being that we are faster, our Mackerel most always becomes our meal." He paused for a chuckle, looked around, sighed and continued. "Can anybody tell me why we are faster than fish?"

Everyone found deep and profound interests in various spots of the cave wall. After avoided eye contact was silence and copious throat clearing. The instructor stepped forth.

"Of course," he laughed "this must be rhetorical. None of you ever wondered why the team with the most Kings and Emperors wins the race every time?" More silence covered the room as Pierre looked around. Not an evasive silence this time, but a curious one. "No?" he paused. "Okay. I guess you don't want to know the secret." Chin up, flippers at his side, the instructor strolled for the mouth of the cave.

Every bird shot up in protest. Begging and pleading for him to continue a lecture they would've once begged and pleaded for him to stop.

One tiny bird in the back over Pierre's left shoulder had a voice that shrieked high above the rest. "Come on! Please tell us. Please! We have to know. I have to know! I'm tired of losing. I can't take this anymore!"

"Okay o-kay, simmer. Simmer yourselves. I suppose I could continue my lecture since you all seem to be so interested."

The instructor clapped his flippers, rubbing them together. "Okay. Everyone lean in. Here it comes."

They leaned so hard Pierre thought they would topple over. The instructor glanced over both shoulders then whispered as if out of breath. "You see, in most cases, when you're talking direct speed, weight in water wins. If you ever want to stand a chance against a team full of Kings, you have to make the course more crooked than straight."

Confusion spread as one twisted expression of stupor met another. The instructor straightened his posture with a proud nod as if he had just shared the meaning of life. "I want you all to remember that, because it's imperative to today's course. While the best tool for finding food may be speed and vision, the best tools for not being it are agility and senses. With that in mind, it's time for today's lesson." He clapped twice more. A chorus of shuffling echoed from outside as rocks clicked and stacked in the entrance. Quickly the outside was going away until the last ray was nixed and they were entombed. Sunlight blocked, the rock-walled room turned to a lightless black vault.

Murmurs crept then jumped into a cracking whine.

"Calm, calm, calm. Calm." Pierre could hear the frown on his face. "Calm yourselves. No one in here is going to hurt you. No one's going to hurt you. But, what if someone was?"

The chatter started again hushed whispers not daring to get too loud.

"Could you do anything? What would be your best chance of making it out alive?" He allowed unease to linger. "To be clear, this is not self-defense. That's ridiculous. That's for someone not trying to eat you. This is survival, and the exercise is designed to teach one very important lesson. If you rely too much on anything, like say your vision, you're a sad story waiting to be told. Imagine this room were an open ocean with an Orca hovering so close his nose could touch your beak. He gets your smell. You're on the run. The water is murky and glum. There's nowhere small to hide. It's getting closer. Closer. Stop!"

They shrieked.

"Most make the mistake of thinking looking back will help them, survive, escape, evade but I'll tell you looking back only slows you down, and I mean that more ways than one. Look ahead. Vision is for what's in front of you, that's why your eyes have their position. Every time you turn to check the negative you lose momentum? Worried more about the fear than freedom of escape."

"I wish I could escape up out of this class right now," a voice said to Pierre's left.

Pounding steps approached through the sand. Pierre leaned back and an angry sound grumbled scarily near, "Mr. Roderick, if you want to survive long enough to have waddlers of your own stop flapping your beak and pay attention."

Pierre found the instructor's hearing, and smell disturbingly acute. Once, a Fairy sneezed and he rattled off her entire diet for the last three months. Told her she needed more krill.

"I'm not aloof," the source getting further away, "most of you would rather be diving off cliffs and chasing fish, I know that, but trust me when I say this is critical. Your predator is ten-times faster than the fastest of you and up to twenty-times bigger than the biggest of you. Nobody ever cares about safety until they feel unsafe but I assure you, you wait until then, and it'll already be too late. Get it, Mr. Roderick?"

"Yes sir," he responded softly.

"Brilliant! Since it's so dark in here that none of you could see your flipper in front of your face, even if you tried, I want you to close your eyes."

Pierre waved his flipper slow back and forth. He was right.

"Cease and desist, Mr. Oiseau. Put it down and bring those eyelids to-geth-er."

Creepy. Pierre squinted.

"To-geth-er," he repeated.

Whoa, he thought and closed them shut.

15

"Thank you. Listen to my voice and feet as I move. This is your guide. When you hear me step left, you step right. When you hear me to your right, move left. When I come closer, hop back. And when I move away, be still. They would only stop hunting if they're tired or lost your scent. Either way, you don't want to reignite their hunger by dragging your odor over the ocean. Give them time to clear out, then go on. Let's begin."

He moved, varying speed and changing direction—sharp cuts, slow steps, stutters, stomps, hesitations, pauses, blitzes, surrenders, lunges, jumps. Shouting and whispering, talking and mumbling. Pierre leaned to the four corners of the Earth.

"This is what it's about young apprentices. You have to feel her. It's all a dance. It's all a dance…"

The classroom wavered away and Pierre fell back to his current reality, alone in the black-blue Atlantic. He replayed the lesson again in his mind while searching for something in the water to free his anxiety. Some logical explanation. Maybe he made a mistake, maybe a school of fish was passing. Maybe a turtle. Turtles swim. Maybe it was gas. Mackerel did give him the bubblies. Maybe_

Grrrrummmmmmmmmmmmmmmmm!

The dark water rumbled, as a large wide cluster of circles rose to the surface. Nothing was visible but few things were certain. This was no fish. This was no turtle. This was not the bubblies.

OISEAU THE KING CATCHER

Chapter 3

A low sound boomed through the ocean, rattling Pierre's core as a dark mass slithered from the deeper layers. Wide eyes followed its enchanted sway as it moved closer and closer to the moonlight. The silhouette formed a husky oval with small fins and eyes that glowed fluorescent green in the indigo setting.

Swim! He tensed. Go! No! Wait! If the creature wasn't after him and he fled, he surely would be then. If it was, and he stayed, nothing could save him. The opportunity was evaporating. What was the move?

Pierre slumped, drifting limply about the surface bobbing with the current. He kept still. The beast thundered. A cold ripple of chills. He kept still. He second-guessed his choice. Now there was no other. The creature pierced a liquid black cloud. A long mass of sparkling silver fur hauled from below. Three times his length. Ten his weight. No hope to outrun.

The leviathan roamed and Pierre closed his eyes nearly shut. Freckled spots stretched across its back and belly. His eyes popped wide. He knew those marks. The patterns of a leopard seal.

Locked teeth were exposed. The flap of flesh that would've covered them was missing. Bubbles escaped Pierre's mouth and ballooned to the surface. The seal whipped to the sound, nostrils flared. Pierre clenched. The seal hovered in a stalk. Pierre's lungs went through a spasm. Not now. The air released was precious, not much was left. His body required him to discharge what was bottled in his lungs and replace it with oxygen. His stomach quivered. He clamped his beak firm. No. He denied his anatomy. Not now, he begged.

Head light, vision blurred and eyelids closing on their own. His stale air was noxious. If he passed out, he'd drown. If he breathed, the beast would swallow him whole. No longer in control, his torso jerked and barrage of bubbles spread into the ocean.

The seal burst in his direction. Pierre leapt from the water, gasping. Splashing back down, the predator raged in pursuit. Pierre tucked his feet close to his tail, and scrunched his neck between his shoulders. He popped his flippers for speed and agility, paddling in quick, desperate strokes. His heart punched through his chest. The world was an aqua-blue blur. A shadow blocked the light and he looked up. The seal rose like smoke then moved fast at a downward angle. Its massive weight spread the water. Pierre rolled. It shot by, snatching liquid. He glanced over his shoulder. The beast rose again, then sunk. Don't look back!

Lunging jagged teeth, it charged. Pierre fanned to stop. It rumbled up in a flurry tumbling him backward.

Pierre was spun in circles. When he got his belly down, he thrust and jet off. Smashing back into the water, the hunter curved trajectory. Aligning with Pierre it swallowed the gap. Heat radiating from its snout was warm on Pierre's tail. He rocked left. The beast snapped. Right. It bit again, nicking flesh. Pierre winced.

The pale moonlight evaporated above. A sharp spike hit in his spine, spiraling him into the abyss. Pierre couldn't stop the momentum. Lower and lower he burrowed. Spinning he looked for the creature. It wasn't there.

Soon Pierre was surrounded by the void, and his eyes were of no more use open than closed. The thick dark down below was ubiquitous, omnipresent, both by his side and in the distance. Dazed, he floated, never knowing what might be swimming with him. What was this? This place where the stars do not touch? Pierre inched in timid commitment. A soft something rolled against his foot. He snatched it close and darted for a spurt. A thump in his throat, eyes large. Noises hummed. He imagined what it could be. Quick taps of crabs scaling rocks, the snap of an electric eel, sleepy, the sleepy strokes of a colossal tortoise. An entire society.

What looked from above to be a vacant chasm was not. This world moved. The sounds around him were strange but welcome.

This bunch, creepy as they were, from all he deduced didn't eat penguin. There was comfort to know he wasn't alone. For now that was good enough.

Taming the jitters, Pierre plotted a course north. He stood no chance hiding in the abyss, and it was not where he belonged. He needed air soon, and he couldn't navigate from here. Cautiously ascending the dark fluid, the noises around shut up. Every living thing abruptly mute. What they left in their place was haunting. The whisper of a soundless pit, following him, making things go away.

Pierre listened in the nothingness as a blinding emerald haze shone bright and sudden as if someone dragged a veil from over the sun. Its stare illuminated the area. Pierre caught in the beam. He turned, grimacing as a clear-lit path sparkled through the ghoulish glow. Pierre shot through the spectrum, out of the dark and so did the creature.

A massive chunk floated in the far reaches. He couldn't make it out. He didn't care. Breaking the surface, he caught glimpses of a strange sanctuary. The leopard seal growled behind, jawing, stretching. Land was in sight. The monster started to porpoise, hopping in and out of the water, drawing close. They arced from the ocean in alternating leaps.

Splish. Splash. Splish. Splash. Splish. Splash.

Pierre was pulling away. The beast cut deep, down to the center of the Earth. Down! Down! Down! Down! Down!

Up! Up! Up! Up! In teleported glitches it bolted from the trenches and a hard pop sent Pierre into orbit. Bursting through the surface, the seal hauled its ten-foot frame into the cold night's air. Its jaw dropped open and half of Pierre disappeared into its mouth. The slimy wet moisture, dripping and lukewarm rubbed against his back. Pierre closed his eyes scrunching into a ball as the teeth rattled shut.

Flailing toward the Atlantic, the beast crashed launching massive waves. Pierre hit next, skipping like a rock across the top of the ocean, violently flipping into different positions each time he hit the surface. Six lashing cycles, and the water went firm. Pierre slid across a smooth surface slamming into a vertical sheet of ice.

Every wisp of wind was knocked from his lungs. A sharp inhale shot knifing pains to his chest and ribs. Twisted in a sprawl, he lay limp on white tundra.

Dawn broke, and as a new sun reflected from the ice everything took an orange-cream color. Figures moved on the horizon and Pierre warred for consciousness. Drooping his head against the hard surface, he heaved a breath and his vision blinked to black.

Chapter 4

Wavering awake, Pierre's body was stretched flat across a firm surface. It was cold. His breaths shallow and constricted. A binding tightness around his chest and stomach made taking in air troublesome as thick bands of seaweed were wrapped tightly around his midsection. *Can I move?* He didn't want to. He tilted his head and found a makeshift bed setting in the corner with a sizeable dent in the kelp. Mixed aromas of supper and stench roamed about. Scanning the small surroundings, he tried to find the source of the smells, hoping one had nothing to do with the other. Before he could land on something enlightening, words were spoken.

"G'mornin' sunshine. It's about flippin' time you woke up. I was getting ready to roll you off and put you back where I found you."

Whoever was talking could not be accounted for.

"Hey!" It griped again, "What do you want me to rub 'em for ya? Get ya webbies out of my face!"

A slap at his left foot revealed sassy yellow eyes glaring up at him. It was a small, well-fed, little-big ol' penguin, about half his size and twice his weight.

Pierre frowned. "Who did I get here and when am I?" he demanded with what he could muster.

"Beg your pardon?" The stranger said.

Pierre sat up and straightened his back from a slouch with sprouting pains. "Mmph. You see what I said, give me some questions or I'm laying down and I'm leaving!"

"Oof, goodness." The portly penguin hobbled toward Pierre. Pierre slid back on the ice. The stranger stopped, stared raised a brow, then coddled something up from under the slab. "Eat the fish."

The stranger threw a sumo-sized piece of meat and it arced over his head.

"Eat the fish." Along came another. "Eat the fish." Then another.

Pierre realized he would eventually get beat senseless if he didn't do as he was told. He caught the next one as it zipped past. It occupied every vacant bit of space in his mouth as both cheeks swelled like blowfish.

"Better?" asked the mysterious host.

Pierre nodded slowly. "Is that chub?"

The penguin paused and frowned. Looked at Pierre, down at his stomach, then back at Pierre. "I may have put on a pound or two since I was hatched, but I'd hardly call it chub."

"No, the fish. Is it Chub?"

"Oh. Indeed it is. Fresh harvest of the Galapagos."

"The Galapagos! Is that where I am?"

"With this weather? Please."

"Then how'd you get the fish?"

"I know a bird who knows a bird."

"Oh."

"But you're not there, you're definitely here."

"Where's here?"

"Nowhere most of the time, somewhere some of the time."

"Which is it now?"

"Most of the time. How I like it."

Pierre's head hurt again, but there were things that needed answering. "So, how did I get here?

"You mean you don't know?"

"No."

"Really?"

"No."

"Really?"

"No!" The shout hurt.

"I thought you would've figured this out by now. Okay, let me see if I can explain. When a mommy and daddy love each other very much they want to express that love you see, and_"

"No. No...No! Not how did I get into the world, how did I get into this place, this cave?"

The short bird exhaled. "Oh, that's easy, I carried you."

"You carried me?"

"Yup." The host focused on a point in the ceiling. "Hoisted you over my shoulder, walking the girth of this island, battling the worst of the elements, fending off predators with my southpaw. Snow up to my hip, and winds! Winds so strong a lesser bird would've been blown out to sea." He dropped his focus. "And it's not a cave, it's a dome."

Pierre vetted the stout figure. "You, carried me?"

"Yeah. What, you don't think I could? It's not all blubber, young fella, there's some muscle under there too," he said, poking his plush body for proof. "Somewhere."

Pierre pursed his beak.

"Okay, I dragged you. Nipped you on the wing, hopped backward most of the way. Stopped a couple times, weather was pretty sunny, and I could see you from my arch, but who cares! What matters is you're in here and not out there."

Pierre wanted to decipher the strange motives but the bottom line was he had been cared for. If any harm were intended, it could've been done already. He relaxed, and muscles unclenched that he didn't know were tense. Cynicism fell aside, as the alluring draws of his appetite climbed. There was more. More to say, more to ask, but Pierre could concentrate on little else for more than a few seconds. Manners implored restraint, but his stomach was turning.

"Fish?" Pierre asked, leaning toward the pile.

"Sure, have as much as you like. I get tons of that stuff."

Pierre plundered the rations, grunting between portions. "I've never been this hungry, and the fish, augh, it's so good." He closed his eyes. Then lifted one open. "You sure this is Chub? This can't be just Chub. I've had Chub and..." Pierre chomped down on another.

"It's Chub, trust me, but anything would taste good after three days."

Pierre half-swallowed and choked. "Three days!" He cleared his throat. "I was out for three days!"

"Give or take, yeah, who's counting?"

"Me! I'm supposed to be in Sud Afrique sun fall today!"

"Well, there's no need to get fluffy. Sud Afrique is just a waddle away from old Bouvet. I'll show you where to depart and point you in the right direction. Grab a couple more," he raised a wing to the sparse supply, "and follow me." The yellow-eyed penguin pivoted half a circle and wobbled out the doorway.

This is Bouvet. Pierre sighed. There's still time to meet aunt and uncle. Slipping off the icy corner of the slab, Pierre teetered in place a bit gathering his balance. The pains in his chest, back, and ribs were subsiding. Swallowing as much food as he could, Pierre stooped under the small exit and hustled to catch up.

Shades of white and celeste reflected from the glacial mountains decorating the skyline and expanse of sprinkled snow. The blank tundra brought with it a foreign calm. Everything here was stoic and still, encouraging him to be the same. The short penguin bustled along gingerly, bobbing his head from left to right. His small strides allowed Pierre to keep pace without much effort. As they walked across the open land, Pierre thought the penguin might say something, but instead he said nothing silence. The lacking exchange was ruffling. A few days ago a little round alien saved his life, helped him to health, offered his home, his rations and now, he didn't even want to know his name.

"What's your name?" the stranger asked.

Oh.

"Pierre Oiseau"

"That French?"

"Guess so."

"You French?"

"No, I'm from East Falkland in the Falkland Islands. What about you?"

"Paul Jaunty. Traveler's traveler, but mainly, anywhere everyone else is not."

"I take it you don't like penguins very much."

"Ya think?" Paul snorted a raspy chuckle.

"Can I ask why?"

"Couldn't hurt."

"Why?"

"Not important. The real question is why a pecker your age ends up stranded and passed out in the middle of my nowhere," Paul said motioning to the icy desert. "What's your story?"

Pierre parted his beak and closed it shut, recall recent events. He opened it again. "There's a war back home between the two islands. It's always been that way and things weren't always as bad as they are now, but they were never good. Time came when bad turned to too bad and my parents sent me to live with some family in Sud Afrique. On my way, I was attacked by a leopard seal, fled, and ended up here."

Paul tilted his neck. "Wow. I don't believe it."

"Me either. Sent alone through a dangerous ocean to a place I'd never been, to stay with family I don't remember. Worse, I don't know when I'll be able to go back, or if," Pierre huffed.

Paul looked at him. "No. I don't believe you wondered why I don't like penguins. Look at you. Thrown from a family to live with strangers because of an age-old fight that had nothing to do with you."

The sincerity brought perspective.

"Trust me, one penguin is fine. Two, mmmmaybe. But once they get in groups it's only a matter of time before they find new ways to destroy each other." Paul shook his head mumbling.

Pierre remained quiet for a while. "If you don't like us so much why'd you carry me back to your cave?"

"Dragged. Dome."

"And get me the fish?"

"I had it."

"And take care of me for three days?"

"Two and a half, and it had nothing to do with you. I was told once we are the sum of our actions. I'm the only penguin on this island. If I walk away you die. I'm tough, but I couldn't live with that. Leaving someone to die should never be an option."

Pierre bounced around the words as they strode, the whistle of the wind mixed with the tapping of claws as they traversed. The island was a hollow hush, equally beautiful as desolate. As tranquil as it was, it felt kind of sad. A type of detachment Pierre never experienced before, and never wanted to again.

"You ever get lonely?"

"Couldn't spell the word. Being alone is a great thing. You get to know the real you. I'll give you an example, I like to pass gas in the ocean." He shrugged. "Go figure. I enjoy the warmth and the bubbles tickle my butt."

The thought crossed Pierre's mind, leaving a sour frown.

Paul lifted his chin. "Ah. The face of a bird who doesn't know what he's missing. Ah. Pity. Point is, it makes me happy. When I lived in a colony I was too afraid of what birds would say. Would they like me, would they hang out with me, would they want to be with me? It was such a waste of time. I know I may be a little funny, I'll admit that, and I may not have any friends. I'll admit that too, but Paul Solomon Jaunty knows Paul Solomon Jaunty."

Paul's brisk choppy steps came to a halt. "Here we are." He bowed. "Swim straight that way and you'll be there in no time." Paul turned and left.

Pierre inched to the edge, leaning over and peering into the liquid.

"It's water," Paul said bending back into the frame. "Ya swim in it."

Pierre exhaled and took a long blink. "I know what it is. Just after what happened, I don't know."

"So what, you're going to live your life not swimming because of one stupid seal?"

Pierre lifted his eyebrows.

"Rubbish. It's one bad time. You can't let that dictate forever. Ya got somewhere to be, the water is how you get there. Boom. Go."

Gazing at the sea in a trance, Pierre touched the seaweed around his waist and took two steps back.

"Okay, okay, I get it. You still got the ooga baboogas. How about this, I'll swim there with you, watch your back. Nobody knows these waters better than I do. I'll make sure nothing happens."

"Thanks," Pierre said softly.

"If you stayed, you'd want to stay with me and I won't sleep in that hole another day. I should be home before dark."

The sun was falling as its rays were being pulled back into the source. A blue-stained sky donned streaks of lavender and amber. Time was growing faint. If he didn't reach that shore by dusk, his aunt and uncle would return to report the news, leaving Pierre in a strange land without a guide. He wished he had a few more days to recover, from everything. Bending to ease himself into the water, he made a faint ripple and slowly flowed away.

Paul charged, grunting and bumbling. Pierre's eyes grew round as sand dollars and the loud smack froze Pierre still. Oh no. Anything with sharp teeth was surely splitting the sea to make their way there for a taste. Pierre turned for land before Paul's stiff beak stuck in his back.

"You focus on the front, I'll cover the rear. We'll have to go above water since I wouldn't recommend you going under for a while. That seaweed around your ribcage is nice for the healing but not really the breathing. You could drown not knowing your own capacity. Didn't do this rescuin' for nothing."

The water sloshed as they separated from the island. The crossing, thus far, was serene. Paul wasn't shy about sharing his thoughts of the pace.

"Are you expecting? I know a Rockhopper named One-fin Willy, swim circles around you. You've got two speeds kid, slow and reverse."

The words chimed as not more than background noise. Pierre was honed straight ahead. So long as Paul was talking, he was still there.

When shore was in sight Pierre swung around to thank Paul for all he had done but the only thing behind him was an empty sea. Paul griped about an aching throat a number of strokes back and said he was going to go mum. Pierre wasn't sure when Paul disappeared, or how long he had been swimming alone. Perhaps Paul Jaunty never meant to take him the whole way but it didn't matter. He was grateful, and a duet of black and white birds stood in the sand up ahead.

Chapter 5

"Pee Pee! Is that you?" the two asked in unison.

He forced a smile. No one called him that in a long time. He wished it would've stayed that way.

"That *is* you! You've grown taller but you've still got that same little beak," his Aunt Patricia exclaimed, batting him on the muzzle. She was a healthy Adelie of strong, defined black and whites that didn't mix or swirl with splashes of yellow from her King heritage. "We told everyone that you were coming! We were getting worried you might not make it."

"She was getting worried," said a thin Magellanic with a long neck Pierre presumed to be Uncle Ferdinand. "I knew a strong swimmer such as yourself could handle what came along..." He paused to examine Pierre's attire. "Hot date?" he pointed to the seaweed around Pierre's chest and gut.

"Oh, I had a run in with a leopard seal. It's supposed to help me get better."

"It's healing kelp? Oh my, are you all right?" his aunt said, shrieking sharply.

"Of course he's all right! Your father's son you are. Did you give 'em the old two to the body, one to the jaw routine?" Ferdinand asked, ducking and fighting an invisible foe.

"Actually I ran like krill. Barely escaped with my life."

"Oh," Ferdinand said slouching. "Well, I guess that's okay too."

Patricia turned with a scowl and chopped Ferdinand in the stomach, folding him in half. Then yelled at his bent over body, "It's more than okay your nephew is safe!" Embracing Pierre, she reminded him of the insanity his uncle was plagued with. "Some penguins love the *idea* of a fight," she said "but wouldn't have a clue what to do if they had to."

Ferdinand emerged from the pale sand catching his breath. "Patricia, I just ate trout. Have you no shame?" Ferdinand caught up and rested on Pierre as they walked. "Sometimes that one still thinks she's in the Falklands," he mumbled.

As they set out for the colony, this new land looked a lot more like home. Sand and gravel in lieu of ice and snow. Greens and grays in place of cold blues and colder whites. The path wound and spun, veered and hooked. The three came to a split.

Ferdinand whispered over his left shoulder, "That trail leads to the forest. Don't ever go there."

Pierre lingered as the myrtle and olive branches stretched out from a winding path paved with a bed of taupe pine needles. The fading light not shining further than a few steps in, as tall, crooked trees bent to cover their domain. Patricia curved them left.

The last moments of warmth emanated from a setting sun as night took center stage. A path of ivory-laid stones, broken in different shapes and sizes met them as they approached the pass. Funneled through statuesque beige mountains, the three eased into a society settling for slumber. Starlight endowed the beach with a luminous glow as the moon left a wide wavering streak both sparkling and majestic on the dark ocean.

A tiny Waddler jumbled into view gasping and giggling, followed by a guardian. A trip, a fall and the chase was over. "I said it was bedtime," the mother decreed, brushing the sand off his body. Tapping her mini on the beak, she nudged him back into a silver and cream dome. Scores of like structures dotted the coast, each filled with the soft rustlings of a day's end.

"Welcome to Caterwaul," his uncle said, "the finest colony on the sea." Ferdinand held his wings out wide with his back to the rolling waves. "Of course the full tour will have to wait till in the morn."

His aunt inquired about his hunger and Pierre respectfully declined. What he wanted most was some voluntary rest. He followed them to the rock they called home and in it was little more than two sleeping spaces made of leaves and pushed together sand. Ferdinand and Patricia showed Pierre to his spot and bid him goodnight.

His aunt pushed the cool sand in closer to his body and pulled a large plush green leaf up to his chest. "First thing tomorrow, we'll send Tiberius to tell your parents you made it safely, but for now, rest." She pressed her forehead against his, then turned and left.

Sleep came like a swift bandit, carrying him into the night.

Chapter 6

As Patricia went to her side of the dome she was practically brimming. Having her nephew arrive gave great joy. In her heart, Patricia admired her brother for staying, and even more so for the reasons that he did. It was honorable, but Pierre being here meant one less penguin flourishing in that morbid hole of death and murder. Caterwaul was a better home, a safer home, a place to have a future and Patricia pledged to keep that true from the day she first discovered the colony.

Through her long voyage escaping the Falklands, Patricia never knew if there was anything across the sea. The sea sort of looked like it dropped off into nothingness beyond a certain point or maybe somehow you would end up in the sky where they touched. She was in search of a large frozen island, not because it was a better island, but because it was the only other island she had heard of. Told to her again and again through a nighttime legend, "Somewhere where the water stops, the ground is cold and hard as rock, a place where most don't dare to go, a place of quiet, still and snow." The story tells of an island where everything was white, where no one could be seen for grand stretches on the clearest afternoons. She wasn't sure it existed. Maybe the story was a metaphor for the celestial nest. Maybe such an island wasn't down here. Maybe so, but she had to try.

When she set out, the massive waves mocked her guile, pushing hard against her strong strokes with gusts of powerful slanted wind robbing her momentum, making her work double. By the time the storm calmed it wasn't dark anymore. Her flippers were moving but her eyes were closed, until something soft swept up under her.

She blinked slow and hard and pulled herself up. The sun was blinding. The sand was twinkling and the water danced of sparkles. This wasn't where she set out to go. Exhaustion cloaked her, inducing a twisted delirium. She couldn't trust what she saw. It didn't feel real. Am I home? Three strangers approached. She stumbled back in her dizzied state and managed to drop them in five moves: stomach, throat, head, neck, ribs, before buckling herself.

When she awoke, there were no less than 20 penguins around her. She popped up waiting to be engaged. They kept a distance. She spun around furiously checking her blind spots until one medium sized Chinstrap stepped forward. "What's your name?" he said in a grungy, commanding tone.

Patricia kept her stance, darting glances to her peripheral. There were many, and not all small. "Patricia," she said, as her voice creaked.

"Well Patricia, I'm the Sachem. I'd like to know why you beat up our medics."

"I thought they were coming to attack me."

"*Attack* you? Why in the Blue Cod would they do that for?" She frowned.

"We don't *attack* penguins in Caterwaul. This is one society. One circle. One crèche. You understand?"

She nodded, so slightly her head barely moved.

"Good. Now walk with me over to the Reserve. We have something to discuss."

Patricia didn't want to go anywhere with him, especially alone, but was in no condition to go back into the ocean, and had no strength to fight 20 penguins. She followed the Sachem, a few paces back, to a giant beige and grey slab. The construct was made up of several pebbles and stones with varying patterns that swirled within each rock. If she ran 30 steps she wouldn't be to the other end.

The Sachem stopped and pointed at the supply. "Eat," he commanded.

Was it poison? Was it free? Was there a choice?

"Eat," he said standing up straight.

Patricia stepped up to the raised slab that kept everything in, as the rim touched above her midsection. She leaned over, picked a piece of plain brown trout so tiny she swallowed it with a small up-thrust of the neck. The Sachem grumbled and etched closer.

"More." He over-enunciated the word, standing over her right should glaring into the pile of cold catch.

She ate another. He nodded. She kept going; four, six, seven, nine. She looked back at the aggressive white face with dark brown eyes. Though Patricia was taller, she felt no ounce of control.

"That's enough," he finally said.

Patricia stepped away feeling slightly more alert. "Are you the head?" she asked.

"As in leader? No such thing. I'm in charge of feeding them, and they respect me for it, but I don't pretend to tell them what they can and can't do."

She swallowed. "How do you all stay safe?"

"From what? You're the only thing dangerous around here. Everything that might hurt us is out there." He pointed to the horizon.

She looked at the landscape. Two caves at each end. One, which extended like a tunnel almost down to the shore and another, smaller cave that sat back about 50 steps from the water. Two gigantic mountains that completely walled and protected the southern half. An expanse of trees that sat high atop the hills before sloping down behind the mountains. It was an oasis. There were small hills, that didn't really look like hills, on the shore with tiny openings.

"What are those?" She asked, unsure if the question was beyond her privileges.

"Those are domes. We sleep in them. Think of it as a small personal cave on the sand. One of our smartest minds built those a while back, but sadly, since then he's left."

He was using more words now. Patricia thought that a positive sign. She wanted to explore the odd creations, but thought better of poking her head in on families after assaulting locals.

"Patricia," the Sachem said coarsely, emphasizing hard on the first three letters. "It is *Pat*ricia, correct?" He did it again.

"Yes."

"Where were you going? When you landed here. Where did you mean to be?"

"I'm not sure." That wasn't entirely true, but she didn't know his motives.

He analyzed her cockeyed.

"Okay. Where did you come from?"

"Somewhere I didn't want to be. Somewhere penguins attack penguins."

"Humm. I see. Well, if you don't know where you're going, and don't want to be where you've been, you're welcome to stay."

A shock snapped through her body. "There's more than enough food, and room, and stuff. Just, dagnabbit, no more beatings!"

She stood completely still.

"You can stay with our friendliest resident. Name's Ferdinand, he's right over there." The Sachem pointed to a row of domes not bothering to specify which one. "If you've had enough fish," he nodded and leaned forward, encouraging her to nod. She does. "Then you can retire. You look awful. We'll reconvene in the morning, and give you the tour. For now, rest." The Sachem walked down the shore so close to the flow that waves rushed him every eight steps.

"Hold it!" She yelled, louder than intended. Citizens within an earshot stopped what they were doing and looked up. "Sorry," she said. They went back to their work.

"Why're you doing this?" She caught up to the Sachem.

He shook his head and grinned. "Because this is Caterwaul, and that's how we are. Stay if you want, or, don't."

Patricia's heart thumped. She cleared her throat. Walking to the domes to search for her host, she broke into a sob.

Recalling the series of events, the locals must've thought she was stark raving crazy. Fighting, yelling, eating, crying. In the following days, Patricia convinced the Sachem that the outside world was dangerous and Caterwaul should set up a system of protection. She wanted this place untainted and unstained. She taught a small force of volunteers how to guard the borders and patrol the landscape. As the group explored the far reaches of the Cape, citizens understood more and more the threats that lie dormant and her number of pupils grew. Patricia took ownership over of the budding force and the little ones started calling her "Safety." She didn't like taking the credit for everyone, but the idea that she could take a bad past and use it for something good was warming and now, she could share this place with her nephew. But for him to remain, something had to take place.

Chapter 7

The following morning arrived a lot sooner than hoped. Rising on the heels of dawn Pierre was awakened by his uncle stammering and making noise about something Pierre desperately needed. He sleepily towed behind the active Ferdinand. They passed his aunt standing in the daybreak, whispering a strange dialect into the ear of a giant bird.

"Is *that* your albatross?" Pierre inquired, more woke.

"Tiberius Flock, in the feather."

"I can't make out what she's saying."

"I'd be surprised if you could. Few penguins speak the old language. It's become somewhat extinct. Which is why we started teaching a more diverse lingo some time ago. Your father can decipher the message, but to most everyone else, it's just gibberish."

"Is that why we're up so early? So I can learn the old language?" Pierre teemed with intrigue.

"No. You need a job."

"A job?"

"Precisely. The colony doesn't have many rules but one the citizens enforce without mercy is the "Contribution Clause." Now come on or we'll miss the whole thing."

Rushing through the gravel, the two stopped at a crowd standing in parallel bunches as if waiting for a parade. Sifting through the assortment of Adelies, Chinstraps, Magellanics, Humbolts, Macaronis and Snares, Pierre and his uncle pushed to the very front before stepping back to move off the trail.

"What's happening?"

"Shh," his uncle said at the same time as a stranger to his right.

Pierre looked where everyone else was looking. A gaping beige aisle.

"No. No! Please!" Pierre heard but could not see "I swear. It was only for a little while. Only for a little while. I didn't *mean* anything by it!" Something being tugged along the aisle cried.

Pierre squinted, the sun's glare obstructing full view. All he could tell was that it was a male, slightly taller than most.

Two Emperors dragged the body without concern. Contorting, the captive jolted himself loose. He crawled over to a citizen and clung to her side, his back to Pierre. "Caroline, please! I was tired. I just needed a break, I was going to get right back. Right back! I was going right back."

The female stared across the way. "I'm sorry. It cost us too much. There's no excuse." She shook him from her lower base, releasing him back to captivity.

The victim kicked and struggled, huffed and struggled, wrung and stopped. Then fought again before being head butted in the temple. Pierre watched from behind the action.

Heads swiveled one after another as what was happening passed their line of sight. Reaching the end of the path, they arrived at the narrow space between the two mountains where Pierre entered the previous night. Ferdinand signaled for them to move closer. Wrestling into position, a pair of slow circling birds in the sky hovered above the captive. Ferdinand stuck a stiff flipper in front Pierre.

The Emperors stopped, and faced the crowd. In alternating turns they spoke.

"Citizens of Caterwaul. You have condemned this being to permanent Banishment," the one on the right said.

"You've deemed him unfit to bask in the pleasures of our society," said the one on the left.

"If any penguin wants to plead on his behalf, now will be your only forum."

"After which, his fate is permanent."

"Thus, any allies to his cause step forward and make your claim now."

Murmurs swelled as the public consensus held court, everyone talking low and rushed. Pierre could only put together pieces. What seemed most commonly said— nothing was left to discuss. The exchanges cordially stopped. Total silence was sustained and more words came from the Emperors on the mount.

"Then the decision is absolute."

They shifted to the guilty party. Something clinched in Pierre's gut.

"Solus, you have been accused and convicted by your equals."

"To be a cancer and a leech upon this community."

"As such, you will be branded as a pariah. Amongst those no longer welcome in this place."

"Return under any circumstances and you will be killed."

"Do you have for yourself any parting remarks?"

By now, the captive had allowed his full weight to fall as a burden to his oppressors. His head drooped, his body hung low, his beak moved with no sound. Pulling himself rigid, the sorrow that embodied him seemed different.

"There will be a cataclysm. A day in which none of you are safe. It will come while you slave, while you slumber. And on this day there shall be no mercy. On this day the tall and the small, those with strength and those without will be together in demise. If you had any notion of what was on the horizon you would consider me wise. Because *it* has already killed so many and now *it* is coming. Toiling in the seas, building on the sand, none of this matters. You will meet your end all the same. And by the time the sincerity of these words comes tapping at your shore, it will already be too late. But. Yet, spare me, and I will do the same. Have mercy, and I will save you. This isn't my last chance. It is yours."

Silence. The lack of sun between the mountains darkened the spot, hiding the prisoner's upper half, but Pierre noticed something sparkle and glint in the shade as he talked. Most of the citizens held firm. Some forced awkward laughs, others whispered. The looming 'what-ifs' were potent.

Both Emperors extract small pointed sticks from slots in the rock and held it in their mouths, carving marks in the captive's flippers. Solus cringed as the sharp wood penetrated his flesh. Replacing the tools, they cawed to the hovering birds above. The sky echoed back and the captive was gone. Escorted into that desolate nowhere from which Pierre had come.

Chapter 8

"What just happened?" Pierre asked, a quake in his tone.

Ferdinand shrugged. "Prophecy, I suppose. Wasn't listening."

"Wasn't listening! He said something was coming!"

"Did he?"

Pierre tilted his head, one eye bigger than the other. *Did I miss something?* He looked around at the Cape, which was eerily settled. No panic, no despair, no wailing for their future. The colony drifted careless as fog.

"You don't actually believe that kook?" his uncle asked, slapping his back. "They're just words of a bird trying to cling to what he had. Penguins will say anything when exile comes, but you can't carry that stuff in your gizzard. Know how I know he was full of guano?"

Pierre gave full attention.

"Why wait?" Ferdinand lifted his eyebrows "Why wait two full seasons until you're about to be thrown out on your tail-feather to tell us we're in danger? A little convenient, don't you think? Could he have said something sooner?"

"I suppose," Pierre said.

"It was all a bargain, a desperate one at that. Hoping if he let us in on his secret, we would let him stay. Which not to mention is ri-diculous."

His uncle cured one question while another took its place. Even if the speech was a farce Pierre still wondered.

"Why couldn't he stay? You have the space." Pierre motioned to the vacant plots of sand. "Doesn't seem like he was hurting anyone. Everyone deserves a second chance."

"He was hurting everybody!" Ferdinand exploded, making Pierre feel small. He turned to his nephew. "If you knew what he'd done, you'd reconsider. Here, we all depend on each other—food, shelter, medical aid, education, protection." Ferdinand started digging a hole with his foot. "If you're not helping us, you're killing us. Literally stealing from hard-working citizens, preying on their labor without giving anything in return. And this is what you become." Ferdinand showed Pierre the hole, it was already deep. "We either fix it, or fall in." Ferdinand filled the void. Stepped back, wriggled his beak, and sighed. "Solus has had more opportunities than there are letters in the word. It was simply his time to go."

Ferdinand tapped his foot, patting the sand smooth, then moved closer to the sea. Pierre was conflicted about how Caterwaul vacated its citizens, but he understood why they needed everyone to do their part. Now, having witnessed what happens to those who didn't, a decision had to be made.

As the audience dispersed, they left in clusters, trudging to their designations. Adults to work and youth to the academy. Not a soul went home. Soon Pierre and his uncle were alone doing nothing and that suddenly felt dangerous.

"You brought me here to show me the importance of getting a job."

"Work or walk, it's the Caterwaul way." He lifted a flipper. "Which, I think given your size, you'd be an excellent Preserver."

Pierre opened his eyes wide and blinked.

Ferdinand nodded. "It's part of what those Emperors were doing. Monitor the shore and sea, protect the residents, show out the unwanted. It's really a do-nothing job, until you have to do something."

Six indentations scarred the sand, three left by each webbed foot of a penguin drug to extinction. Pierre's stomach got warm. Everything he needed to know about a Preserver's duty was shown moments ago and the thought kicked up billows in his conscience.

Ferdinand and Pierre left to consult with Patricia, and caught her scurrying out of the boulder.

"D.E.W!" she shouted, running away. "Give your wounds time. Figure what you want to do," she turned to backpedal, "good luck," she smiled. Faced with the ultimatum, he took her up on her offer.

His uncle pointed him in the direction of a dim cavern on the far side of the cape. He stooped to fit under the passage, and was met by something small and energetic.

She spoke in rapid whispers. "Welcome to the cavern of the D.E.W. Are you dropping off or picking up?"

"Neither," Pierre said, matching her tone, "I'm here for a job."

She looked Pierre up, and down, and then back up. "As what security? You're a little big to be a D.E.W. aren't you? Sure you don't want to be a Preserver?"

"Positive. I'd rather work here. My aunt Patricia said it'd be good," Pierre said, not fully sure where here was, but figuring it had to be better than there. He heard the term back home a few times in passing. He wasn't told what it was, but a lot of pretty penguins worked there and little more needed to be known.

"So *you're* the new one. There had to be one. The way they heaved Solus out of here like that."

Pierre was lost on how to process the statement. He cracked his beak to speak but the words came out of hers. "After he'd been slacking for this long I asked myself why now? Why is this all of a sudden his judgment day?"

She looked at the wall, shaking her head and muttering. Then back to Pierre. He blinked. She stepped to his stomach.

"But that's neither here or there. So you, o' leviathan seabird, want to be a Designated Egg Watcher?"

A breath drew from Pierre as he imagined every modicum of his masculinity exiting the room. He yearned to follow. His jaw slipped ajar. No bravado was to be found in the profession. I'm a Tee-Waddler, I'll be courting soon, they will want to know what I do. I can't tell them I'm a big nanny. He prattled over his words peering out of the cave.

He caught the attendant's smirk before she tucked it away. He refused to give the satisfaction of him running, flippers flailing, screaming like a coward. The only way to regain his dignity was to act as if he still had some.

He coaxed his composure, and spoke with as much bass as his maturing throat could muster. "Yeah. I know penguins like me don't usually do this type of stuff but I figured it was about time to give these eggs some uh — masculine tenderness."

They shared a long pause. It would have been better not to talk at all. She retreated from his midsection.

"Hmph! If you're eager to serve then who am I? My name is Sherri, I'll show you what we do." Leading Pierre deep into a secluded inner sanctum, she unveiled the backend of the cave.

A cocoon sprinkled with a couple dozen eggs stretched a fourth of the space. Some white and oval-shaped, some yellow and more circular. Some were metallic grey and others a faded burgundy freckled with splashes of obsidian and neon green.

"These are the future trouble makers of Caterwaul," she said. "Now what makes a good D.E.W is fierce attentiveness. You have to anticipate the needs of the penguin-to-be."

What needs? It didn't require a light jog, it was an egg. An egg that hadn't even hatched. It was an unhatched egg.

"Every so often you have to come back here and check their temperature. Place the back of your flipper on the median of the egg. If it's too warm, rotate it to a cooler plot. Too cold, warm it with your brood patch. Our life gives them life."

She paced the room, methodically nursing. She motioned for him to do the same. "The regulation of heat keeps them somewhere between liquid and ice." Sherri wheezed a cackle to her own dark humor as she shook her head and scooped a small lime colored oval onto her toe knuckles. Lifting her upper half, she slowly melted a warm bare patch of skin at the base of her gut over the egg and relaxed. "But seriously," Sherri continued, "there's nothing I value more than these eggs, especially with there being so few. This room used to be filled with all kinds of joy, but now, all we've got this corner. Which is why I guard them rabidly. No tolerance. You hurt my little chirp-chirps through intention, or neglect…and I'm coming." She spied the new help. "You hear me. I'm coming."

Pierre looked left, frowned, nodded.

"Mmhmm," she said, "get warmin'. Third one in the second row is always a bit chilly."

Pierre moved to the position and sure enough it was frigid. He didn't have a brood patch, those come with parenthood, but he mimicked her motions. When he got to a cold one he'd hunch over and give it a quick rub against his tummy 'til it was warm enough to set back down. He knocked over a few, sat on others, and placed three or four upside down, but with repetition his blunders evaporated. The two completed their rounds and returned to the front as the swelling temperature met them at the mouth of the cave. A bright late morning with warm wind and radiating sand. The growing heat caused much fuss with his instructor, and she griped as if just being dropped in this hot place today. After much talking and exacerbated sighs, she moved seamlessly into the gossip of the Cape—who chose who for the upcoming mating season, which ones really let themselves go, and who may be taking care of an egg that isn't theirs. Who's been talking mess and who's been doing it. Sherri required absolutely no response to hold a full conversation.

Pierre presumed why some birds back home flocked here in droves. The damp hole was a hotbed of the wet gossip. A place where they could sit in the shade and barter their speculation. He understood the appeal, but the vacant hearsay had no draw on him.

Shifting to the outside world, he watched the sun intently. Hoping it'd hear his plea. Trudge faster. Trudge faster!

Through the chatter Pierre caught a whiff of something like self-awareness.

"Am I talking too much? I hope I'm not talking too much. Do you think I'm talking too much? Because I don't think I'm talking too much."

Sherri continued to ramble as he stood in the archway, invariably mute. Nothing to add, nothing to subtract, nothing to rebut, slowly drained by endless noise.

She stood from her spot in the sand and finished a thought, "And she knew that wasn't his egg all along. I tell ya, that Bessie is triflin' 101. I'm going out to the Reserve. Haven't been able to get to lunch since the last twelve assistants left."

"*Twelve?*"

"Twelve. And ain't none of them worth a bit of nothin'. This used to be an operation overflowing. Guess the eggs were just too much. You can handle the rabble-rousers on your own for a while, right?"

Pierre nodded intensely.

"They won't bite. You want something? We've got Cod, Caper, Goby, Blenny, Smelt..." before Pierre could respond Sherri had talked her way down to the beach.

He stood at the edge of the cave, more relieved with each step she took. The day's sparkle was on the ocean. A warm breeze brushed across his face, reminding him so much of home. It wasn't hot. It was perfect, the heat luring him out of the cold. Pierre resolved, in that moment, he must escape. Slipping into the back room, with his devious plan, he gathered some eggs. Sooner than hoped, the sound of webbed footsteps crunching sand echoed from the entrance. He adjusted what he could and got into position.

Chapter 9

Marooned on a vaguely island, Solus scraped cold collections of snow from his chest and wing. He felt a burning as he grazed the fresh gushing scars on his shoulders. The marks were mysterious, much like the penguins who put them there. But not understanding their translation didn't keep him ignorant of their meaning. He was the newest member of a group as old as civilization itself—the shunned, the unwelcomed, they who do not belong. Amongst the cursed ex-citizens, purged from the place they call home, sworn to be killed on sight if ever they dared return.

Though the ever-present threat loomed over Caterwaul since inception, for an actual Banishment to occur was rare. There were only four others like him that he could remember, three of which he heard had since moved on to the Celestial Nest. Given the larger population, Solus was in small company.

Squinting, he surveyed the island, pestered with the strange inkling he'd been here before. To his left and his right stretched a bare canvas unpainted. A tundra tinted by passing reflections. Orange from the sun, light and dark blues from the ocean and sky, and white from the continuously falling snow. Some might make a mistake and call this place beautiful. But Solus saw it for what it truly was. The shades came and went, with the land having no control over when, or how or why. The land only vibrant under another's glow. Only illuminated in the presence of other light. No true shine. No color to call its own. Its bare nature was hollow. And although Solus still wasn't quite sure if he knew this place, somehow, it reminded him of when he was young.

The sand beneath his claws was the only thing his father stayed long enough to leave a good mark on. Everything else went untouched. Solus spent more nights than his small mind could count standing at the doorsteps of the Atlantic, hoping the tide would wash in more than foam and knots of kelp. Seasons bled together and warm became hot, hot became cold, and cold became freezing. Somewhere in the midst of all that waiting and all that wanting Solus stopped wishing. His hope hardened several times over as disappointment and disdain were as sure to come as the rising sun. Absence nested in place of affection, and kindled a loathing to overthrow longing. Anger flourished with each passing year as he built his strength and started searching, going farther and farther from the Cape. Looking no longer for love, that time passed, now he wanted something more appropriate. Revenge.

The fiery orb up high burst through a gap in the clouds and lit up the ice. Solus saw a small lump in the distance. Too small for a mountain and too large for a rock, curving up from the flat surface. The sun hid again and visibility fell to overcast and a flurry of snow. As always the light was fleeting and circumstantial. Restricted and temporary, but darkness can be found anywhere, even in the height of day. There was value in that. The only thing trustworthy is consistency. Right or wrong, at least he'd know what to expect. That was all he could ask.

Aligning with the vision, Solus dug his long jagged claws into the hard ice for traction. Smiling wide, he marched.

Chapter 10

"What the flip are you doing!" said a heavy voice.

Pierre smothered a smile. He jostled in place, moving eggs around, adding flare to his performance. Paces pounded around, prickly pebbles of sand chipped at his body. This was better than imagined. Staying blind was becoming less doable as temptation pulled. Cracking a lid to enjoy Sherri's expression, he caught the physique of a robust Emperor mother. A seething glare shot from the dark violet eyes. She was bigger than he was. Joy turned to fear. He was paralyzed. *That's not Sherri.*

"Get your fat head off my egg!"

That's not Sherri. Pierre rushed to his feet, apologizing, stumbling, as the mother clutched her offspring between the tip of her wings and stormed out of the cave. Pierre followed to the archway, explaining, expressing. She stomped to the water's edge, and talked lively to another penguin. They both turned toward the cave. Pierre pinned himself to the inside wall. Possibilities swam through his mind. He peeked around the corner. They were coming. He retreated to the back of the cave and started rearranging his mess. The females thundered into the room.

"That's him!" the larger one shouted.

Pierre swallowed so hard his beak clicked.

"He was using my Leviticus for neck support!"

"Is that true?" Sherri asked in her calmest tone of the day.

"Sort of, but I wasn't really resting on it. Just acting like it."

"Why?" Sherri asked.

"Because I thought it was you coming back."

"What difference does that make?"

"I wanted you to let me go."

"You just got here!"

"I know."

"Why?"

"Honestly, you talk too much."

Sherri shifted her weight and took in a big breath.

"He ain't lyin'!" her accomplice shouted. "Sherri, you know you can talk. That beak just run like the river. Flippidy flap flap flippidy flip!" The Emperor penguin mother walked up on Pierre. Her purple eyes wide, her smile large making him uneasy. She laughed. He laughed too. She stopped. Pierre shut his mouth.

"Next time you want out of something, use another egg." She brushed some sand from his shoulder.

He flinched.

Sherri bounced focus between the two, settling on her subordinate.

"Why the hoopla, why didn't you just quit?"

"I wanted to quit the minute I found out what a D.E.W was, but I was embarrassed. And then I didn't also want to be a quitter. So, for reasons you may not understand, I needed you to let me go."

Sherri paused. "Get the hell out of my cave."

"Thank you, Sherri. Thank you. I'm sorry." Pierre left. His small degree of remorse was burned through like the morning fog when he stepped into the sparkling sun and his world came to life. Whooshing waves, cawing gulls, other penguins, he was never so happy to be fired.

Chapter 11

Finishing his first dip of the day, Paul Jaunty wiggled dry and waddled back into his home. He lingered near the archway in a wide stance as he relished the reclaimed solitude. This place which had given so much. When Paul first came here for asylum, he felt like a hypocrite. He prided in telling his impressionables that if they could see it, and scheme it, they could build it. But it had to be built in the mind first before it could exist in this world. He'd given so many lectures. Lectures on adaptability and creativity; problem solving and using your resources. The irony of the former Builder wandering homeless made him feel false. Like one who was a master of theory but nothing else. What happens when life doesn't give you materials to build with? He used to have a crew, tools, time, assistance. In a place like this, that offered true independence and isolation, the answer loomed beyond his craftsmanship.

When he fled home he did it in such a panic it slipped him how this former tool could provide a refuge. A curious shell clicked together through altered blocks of compact snow. Squares, rectangles, rhombi, circles, trapezoids, parallelograms, and other shapes that had no formal name but were needed to make it work.

A relic assembled well before they traversed this great plain, which came like the blessing of Prometheus.

At first, they didn't know what to do with it. Initial experiment was as follows: One crept up in front of it, squawked, then waddled off and ducked behind a small rock. After a few sessions of provocation, they moved to grander studies. Probing the exterior. The penguins beat their wings alongside the round base, listening for a response. Nothing. Progress was lethargic and likely would've remained that way until instinct revealed a purpose.

Caught in one of the many malicious snowstorms that plagued the island, a combination of damp frost and whipping wind threatening to freeze their eyelids shut, the birds shuffled themselves into the round space. Although the hole in the top let in some of the harsh outside, they found themselves much better off and greatly protected. The storm passed, roaring to terrorize another locale and the small company hesitantly emerged. As they turned to look at the structure, devoutly intact, its use was clear.

Set on reconstruction, their drastically different landscape offered many challenges. Physical and environmental obstacles were discouraging along with the nagging questions. What to build with, who to do it with, and how? Many sized it up as an impossible task, the most optimistic called it impractical, but the ones on the island that day with Paul didn't have the luxury of being oblivious. They were spared in its hollow. This wasn't fantasy, it wasn't lagniappe, this work had purpose. They didn't know what they were doing. It had never been done, they only knew that it needed to be. Why? They didn't know that either.

But stubborn faith is infectious. Maybe believing in something hard enough for long enough appeared to give it some particle of truth. The more the four devoted themselves to the pursuit, the more intrigue that surrounded if they could really do it or not. Citizens began to talk. Some offered to help, others offered their opinion. The group's resolve was growing and unflappable, there was a reason for this discovery, a reason they were there a reason for the storm.

Trolling the shores for building material was exhaustive. The effort almost never made it off the ground until one day a treasury of talc was discovered by a bird Paul grew to fancy with a spirit for exploration. The soft rock-like substance was prone to manipulation, and could be cracked with a striking blow. A substance brittle enough to be broken but sturdy enough not to crumble under weight, Caterwaul found its ice. The 'what' was solved, the 'who' was implied, but the 'how' was still a mystery.

How to stack these broken blocks in a structure? They couldn't lift them and they needed help. A barter was made with the local neighbors. Food for help. After a week of proving the birds could source enough plants to feed them, the tree dwellers got to work.

The Cape looked like a wasteland of misshapen white rock, dotted across the shore. Workers in other fields grew impatient, disapproving of the new industry and the mess it made of their home. For all the completed collapses and others that toppled daftly in early stages, one stood. Unshaken by climate or force. The triumph had emerged, and in the shadow of their success the Cape was colonized with its children as their Darwinism dawned.

The accomplishment sparked a growth, one from which Paul would never see their kind digress. The first, affectionately called Le Pere de Tous, was the place Paul now regally inhabited. The master mold, which spawned all others.

The structure that taught them how to build and inspired them that cold stormy day was now his home. The opening in the roof was seen as a structural flaw back home, something to be fixed and closed off, but Paul thought it was the best part. He didn't care much for day, it was bright and bothersome, haunting in fact, but the night held sparkles that dropped into the circular space, making a bluish glow. He watched the constellations because he wanted to, but also, to know she was there.

In the long twelve seasons since her incident, Father Time had yet to do his one good job. The pain still pulsed powerful as ever. Crawling from self-pity and self-loathe was a process with which he hadn't made much traction. Staring through the northern void, he located what he sought and sank.

Pyxis, the mariner's compass. She was his guide in this life and in the next still the same. Paul never wandered far from that brief straight string of stars that reminded him of who he once was. When the freshness of the world hadn't yet started to fade, they would lie in the sand on a cool night and she'd point out clusters with the number of waddlers she wanted. Each star represented an egg. Her first choice, had fourteen. Paul nearly fainted, waiting for a comforting joke, or laughter, or a sly look, or something. None came. Later he found out she was kidding, but it wasn't until much later. Paul guessed that was her way of making sure he was there to stay, no matter what. After many polarized debates the two settled on Pyxis, which showed itself early that autumn, days before they were officially Bonded. Paul had a life rule. He never wanted more penguins than toes, and was happy to find Pyxis only had three stars.

His partner was a cartographer. Her duties took her on perpetual exploration, far from the settlement. When she returned home, her primary obligation was to sketch images of her discovery into a soft stone slate while fresh in her mind. Paul didn't know what to do when she was gone. He submersed himself in his craft, working far into the night. Following one trip that took longer than usual, she couldn't stop talking about a large monster sitting atop the water. Over time, the monster got closer and everyone could see. The object was gargantuan, alien, and statuesque. She spent plenty of time out at sea, studying the form. When home, she headed straight for the map, marking what she found. Every time she returned her feathers were a bit more dull and a bit more colorless. The black and white made way to grey and the Wellness Ward said they'd never seen it before. It wasn't their fault, Paul reminded himself. It wasn't their fault. They were accustomed to dealing with flesh wounds and marks from predation but what this was worse. It was as if something wilted her from the inside, stealing everything except her life. Then it took that too.

That was the end for Paul. He didn't care about building anymore. He didn't care about the Cape. He wanted it back. He saw reminders in every detail of a place that was once their own. Without warning, one morning, Paul left.

In front of him now, neatly sculpted into a section of the wall, was a series of arcs and curves that came together to make a portrait of an Adelie. An elegant mural, best by night. Crooning his neck he carved corrections, weeping softly, as he touched the ice and mourned for their broken bond.

The light disappeared from the doorway and a voice crawled into his ear. "She's beautiful," something said beyond the arch.

Paul swung around. What crept in from the darkness had beady round optics, the size of small pebbles. Its pupils dug far into the skull and a blood-red radiance made looking into his eyes like staring down the vent of a volcano.

Paul staggered. "Ravaillac!"

"Oh, Paul, must we be so formal? Please, call me Solus."

Chapter 12

Tiberius would never forget the first time Patricia approached him. "I need a bird to do something dangerous," she said. The appropriate response would have been curiosity. Followed by questions, a give and take on what made it dangerous, where he was going and why she didn't do it herself. Was she asking because she too thought he was disposable? So if it went south they could shrug their shoulders and consider themselves lucky they didn't lose someone *really* important? Those were the questions he should've asked, the process he should've followed but instead he said nothing but yes. It wasn't even something to be answered in the negative or affirmative, but he didn't care. He wanted her to know, whatever it was, whatever he had to do, he was her bird.

The opportunity to work for the most influential being in Caterwaul was a chance to upgrade his place on the caste system. A positioning that brought status, notoriety, and a way of pride. He was no longer an albatross, he was Patricia's Trans-Atlantic. That meant something. The unmeasured risk was mild compared to the sure ridicule he was bound to suffer if he stayed as he was. Living as an awkward oaf who hadn't proved good for much more than comedy. He could never outrun the opinions of his oppressors, he had to stand above them. And they would never accept him as their equal, because he wasn't. A normal life wasn't attainable. That was a gift denied. Every other visitor who had come to that year's pool of fliers sighed, shook their head, and looked at him with such big pity he felt pity for their pity. By first nightfall, his only remaining company was the sick and crippled. He thought he would be shooed away with the others until someone approached so quietly, for a moment, he didn't know anyone was there. She was average height and very quiet. She nodded toward his wings. He stretched them for her, far and wide but could barely hold them up. She pointed for him to run. He took four steps, wobbled and fell. She tapped her throat, signaling him to caw. What resonated was a shrilled yip. She smiled. Not saying a word.

As the rushing wind parted the tip of his beak en route home from the Falklands, Tiberius wondered what it would be like if he had refused. He saw his future as a long dim corridor down a hollow dripping cave. He was the worst at sprinting short-distance, and had no talent for extraction. If he couldn't make it as a Messenger, he had no other value to the Cape. Patricia gave him what no one else would: a right to be there. Without which, he would be much like Solus.

OISEAU THE KING CATCHER

Chapter 13

Bothering a few Humbolts working on the shore, Pierre learned of his aunt's whereabouts. For reasons unknown, she was sort of famous. Before he described what she looked like, they called her by first name and pointed impatiently down the way. At the mouth of a gaping hollow, far into the mountainside, Pierre was greeted by several of her faces, etched into pillars. Dramatic profiles, chin lifted, pondering into the distance. He approached the closest one. Below, the inscription read: Patricia Oiseau – The Safety of the Cape.

Pierre guessed this academy was the same as back home. A place the young went for G.E. before being assigned a career. Though what was taught surely had to be different. Their basic courses were combat training. Here, it might be arithmetic. The entrance was on a mild slope, and pools of water collected when the tide washed in. The stationary saline trapped against the rock, chewed holes to the left and right causing small, pumpkin-shaped cavities. A rumbling call echoed through the hallway and swung Pierre around to floods of Wee-Waddlers pouring out of their prisons, bumbling toward the beach. Jubilant masses parted him at the midsection.

Patricia trailed the crowd, looking mildly surprised to see him standing there like a rock in a rushing stream.

"Sherri?" she asked.

He nodded apologetically.

"Figured. She could talk through her own funeral. Nobody can stand it for too long, but I was hoping you'd at least make it through the day. For your wounds."

"I'm fine," Pierre responded, looking down and off. Patricia jabbed him with a stiff poke. Pierre forcefully cleared his throat. She circled around the green bandages, and stabbed him with another. It would've hurt regardless. Why was she so strong? Like, for what reason? Pierre winced while she was behind him, but held a straight face when she was back in front.

"See," he gritted, "she healed them."

His aunt let out a startling bright laugh. "Impressive then! We should put her in the Wellness Ward."

"No, she is unbearable."

"Sherri's irregular but she provides a valuable service. Not many have the patience to sit all day warming the unhatched. If it weren't for her, a lot of us would not be free to do what we do."

"Still."

"If you had to be in a cave, dark and lonely, you would sniff out things to entertain yourself too. Now come, we have stuff to discuss."

Patricia motioned toward the opening, led Pierre out and watched her students. As the two moved further from the mouth, the sound of soft crunches of sediment met with rambunctious youth at play.

"You've been through a lot at your age." She said walking in slow, sure steps. "Our more…troubled pupils at the academy could use your experience. To help them make sense of their lives and some of the things that's happened. I was thinking, it could beneficial for everyone if you spent some time as a counselor."

Pierre looked up.

"They're at such a transitional stage." She led him to a spot in the shade. "They won't be waddlers much longer, soon they'll be in the thrust of adolescence. You about to come out of that might offer something to help them make their way."

Pierre stepped into the sun. A shadow swept over from above. Patricia brayed and Tiberius dropped hard to her side. The albatross donned a white chest of neatly groomed feathers that transitioned into cherrywood wings and a dark aureolin beak. He fluttered, tucked his wings, and the two once again started their incessant whispering. Patricia giggled something into his ear. The albatross half-turned, shook his head, and turned back. It didn't take telepathy to know his occupational theatrics would soon be Trans-Atlantic news. His mother might chuckle about the eggs, a bit, but his father would find no humor at all. He felt the cold paternal stare from across the ocean. His parents risked a lot to get him to safety and repaying them with shenanigans and sheer lack of respect was beyond explanation.

His aunt walked by his side and nodded to Tiberius as he bolted into the air. The gust pushed Pierre back in the sand but Patricia stood firm.

"Made a decision?" she said, turning to her nephew.

Pierre stepped forth. He understood the rationale, and concern for her students but how could the blind lead the blind? He was unsure and out of place. A temporary fixture in this new world, that would leave quickly as he came if ever called home. It was wrong to forge this trust with a presence so fickle. In all, he wasn't qualified to be responsible for someone else. He pursed his beak.

"Well, I won't force. But know that when you're ready, there are many of us that could really use you. Just don't live under your potential forever. You're more than an egg watcher." She smiled. "In the meantime, if you're any good on the chase you can try your luck at your old job."

Pierre stared, befuddled. "How do you know about my old job?"

Patricia revealed an omniscient grin. "A birdie told me. If you're going, you'd better hurry. The sun is at its height, so it's nearly roll call." His aunt nipped the end of the now-stale seaweed, unraveling him in big loose circles. "You don't want them to think you're a liability."

Regaining his equilibrium after the series of twirls, Pierre caught his bearings and scurried off.

"They'll have hard enough time trusting you as is," Patricia muttered, watching her brother's son.

Chapter 14

Solus paced side-to-side examining keepsakes: withered flowers, sea stones, and a pile of neatly laid kelp. Paul stood silent, afraid to interrupt an intrusion of his own home. Solus' jagged claws slid back and forth.

As the Fiordland slithered near a certain spot, Paul spoke up. "What are you doing here Ra...umm...Solus?" He patted the edge of his beak.

"Searching."

"For what?"

"Answers to questions I haven't yet learned to ask."

The cryptic response did little to clear confusion. Three years had gone by since Paul had seen the bird stalking about his home. Solus held a distant and disturbing nature even back when he was his pupil at the Builder's Academy. To be accepted into the department, students had to display superior cognition in all three fields of intellect, motor skill, and T.D. communication during their time at the academy. The requisites were nonnegotiable, and Paul made no exceptions. Constructing a living environment was a beautifully dangerous task. Caterwaul was one of the few places bold enough to even try it. He wanted to be sure they understood the risk.

Paul would take his students to Bouvet Island several times throughout the year to study form and apply this ancient knowledge to their projects back on the Cape. He was stiff, and not without bias, but always fair. The potential peril made him impatient to error. One piece out of place, one block not chipped to form, and the dome could crash with the family in it. It was an honor, not a right or a privilege. Most students were so proud to get accepted they were bouncing when he delivered the news. Anxious to join the core of penguins who would literally build a better tomorrow. Solus was different.

Whenever he bothered to stop by the outdoor lectures, he sat in the closest spot to the ocean, quietly and permanently fixed on the never-ending sea. Whenever class was in the cave, he walked in, looked around, turned and left. There was no way of knowing for sure how much information actually sank in. Whenever Solus was asked a question, he'd answer the question with another.

How many builders does it take to assemble a structure? How many to take it apart? What are the strengths of using a thirteen-stone base system? What are the deficiencies? What makes us Builders important to the colony? Why are they important to us? And so it would go, every session Paul was vexed with his presence. A lust for knowledge was encouraged, but he secretly dreaded Solus' curiosity.

"Any visitors lately?" Solus asked, breaking Paul's trance.

"Why would you ask that?"

"I noticed a small dent in the far corner. Only a shape like yours could make such a short but wide hole, and I thought, that's strange. Why not sleep where you were meant to sleep? Why in the corner of your own home?"

"Well, sometimes I—"

"No, no. That wasn't a question." He paused, still and rigid, examining his old professor. The round bird felt Solus inching up every part of his being with the crimson stare.

"When I invited myself in and stepped into the light, I saw an entirely different indentation here on the bed." Solus pointed to the elevated slab in the center of the room. On it, was an impression twice as tall.

"Something quite larger than yourself, and I became curious. So I'll ask again. Have you had any visitors lately?"

Paul tried to deduce what Solus would want with that information, or why he cared, but while he didn't know his motives one thing was certain—there wasn't a well-wishing feather on his body.

Paul stole a glance at the raw engravings carved into each wing. Deep markings revealing whitish-red flesh meat. The scar tissue was bubbled to the surface. Solus was not away from the home by choice. Banishment made the Fiordland more than disturbed, more than dangerous, it made him desperate. A bird with no home was one waiting to die. Paul knew that better than most.

Solus paced patiently, again scanning the walls as Paul shifted in place.

"Just an old friend," he finally managed. "From an island over, come to pay me a visit. Nothing spectacular."

Solus pivoted sharply, bent his neck, and smirked. "A friend. From an island over. Come to pay you a visit." he let out a chuckle that sounded like a growl. "You were a hopeless recluse even before you lost your poor Felicia."

"Flora." Paul stiffened. He was instantly sorry. There were few things he was afraid of, and death ironically was something for which he developed a torn longing, but this was different. Solus had no cause for vendetta. No reason to seek him out after all this time. True, Paul had him removed from the program, but with Solus having more freedom in his next position, ultimately Paul thought he did him a favor. No, if this were about him there wouldn't be this dancing, this moving, this game. If he were here to kill it would've been done already. No. Paul recognized he was just a tool. Substance being manipulated for purpose. For what? He could not be sure.

Solus crumpled a pair of vibrant yellow brows at Paul. "Flora, of course, forgive me. I too was offended. A friend from an island over," Solus scoffed. "We both know you have no visitors." He touched the slab in the center of the room. "Bouvet is the most, and perhaps only, used rest point for travelers going to the Cape. Void of predators, plenty of food, and known for its festivities. During its off-season this place is a funnel for all things headed to the 'greatest colony on Earth'." Solus projected through the hole in the roof. "Thus, if a new bird went into that Cape it likely would've come through right here," he sneered. "As a mapmaker's widower you know this. So for a friendless, loveless, loner, such as yourself to claim company from an island over is very *very* insulting," Solus grumbled, gritting his beak, stepping closer. "No one visits you. Just me, just now."

Paul was pinned against the wall, highlighting the difference in size. Pressed flushed against Flora, he gasped in the shadow of a towering frame. Paul's strength left in fluctuations.

"Instruct me, professor." Solus scowled, speaking down to the top of his head. "I crave your knowledge. Tell me who you've been harboring and I'll be on my way."

Sliding his foot back an inch, Paul felt the thud of his heel hit the solid wall. Nowhere to go. The intruder was faster and stronger than he in every way, entering the physical prime of adulthood while Paul was slumping into the twilight of his life. The small penguin stilted the quiver in his body, swallowed the tremble in his voice and parted his beak. "A friend," he said, barely above a whisper.

Solus probed Paul. Fiery eyes shot back and forth Paul's face, acknowledging every twitch, every squint, every flinch. Solus tilted his neck to the left, peeking behind Paul, and marched toward the door.

"Let's try this another way," Solus said, throwing the words back over his shoulder. "Remember your lecture on cornerstones?"

Blood left Paul's face as Solus vanished into the dark.

Chapter 15

After tripping twice, Pierre sloshed to a stop next to four blotches in line. They were rigid and stern. Preliminary detail had started.

A Chinstrap with narrow eyes and square jaw stomped in front of the group. Starting with the penguin at the far end, he issued commentary on yesterday's expedition. "Xander! You're faster than a shark late for work. It's why I let you Spear opposite me on the hunt. But precision comes from poise, and knowing when to use that speed. Timing makes the team. It *is* the team and your impatience is a liability. One costing us precious catch."

Xander nodded hard adjusting his posture, making it straighter than it already was. Pleased with silent compliance, the leader slid down the row. Pierre nudged the Magellanic to his right. He nudged him once. He didn't move. Twice. No reaction. The third time Pierre pushed him into a brief stumble. The penguin peddled back into his stance and shook his head.

Their instructor moved down the line, pausing in front of a bird that hadn't missed any meals.

"Puddles! I don't know how many times I have to tell you! Our job is to catch for the colony. Not eat for the colony. Yet ev-e-ry time we go out, you bring back more in your gut than you do with your beak! You've been a Straggler from day one, and today, nothing has changed."

Pierre checked. He was two away.

"Aria! Masterful execution. Incredible technique. Improve your jousts, and you can have Xander's spot."

"Yes, Sachem," a voice replied in a clear, soft tone.

Pierre leaned to take a look. The commander shot him a glance. He snapped back.

"Cole! Great work. You're a reliable bird," the foreman said to a boxy Galapagos, before stepping in front of Pierre. Gazing at his cast, he slanted sideways and whispered low, "You are not sly. You are not slick. I don't know who you are, and I'm not sure if I should care, but the last bird that held that spot let us all down. So, you could be slow as a manatee in mud and have the experience of an egg but you had better, better be loyal. You abandon us and you can forget about Banishment. I will shove you into the jaws of an Orca myself. Or should I say seal?"

Pierre sprung a look into his obsidian rounds, hoping for banter or farce but instead only found a discomforting sincerity. No grin, no wink, no inkling of the disingenuous.

"Don't worry," Pierre responded. "I couldn't leave if I wanted to."

The commander's face shrank. A concentrated clump glaring at Pierre. "Good," he said, looking up. "Good."

Chapter 16

Where was safe? Inside or out? Solus' parting remark lingered like a dark foretelling of things to come. The irony was, it was a dome structure. There were no corners and thus no cornerstones, which would be good, except not having a cornerstone actually made every base block of equal importance. You could attack any shape at the bottom row and start to collapse a home. The silence was taunting. Outside was still. Paul wasn't convinced of any deep breaths or quick motions. The small bird dreamt a dream that it all went away. That his aggressor decided he was telling the truth.

It was silly. Nearly every known colony sleeps on their webbed feet in the capricious elements. While the seabirds of Caterwaul graduated to shelter, others filled their days with base survival. Each one for his or herself. Caterwaul managed a division of labor. Progress in jumps, spawned from the notion that some do stuff better than others, and should be allowed to concentrate on that for the benefit of all. Departments created to nurture intellect, tend to potential, and capitalize on skill, for broader advancement. Modernization salted their pallet. Simply living became extinct. Schools restructured to teach more than how to catch food and not be it. They lusted for a deeper understanding of themselves, the world around them. How to fix a sick body, and overcome limitations. They pushed. Not stopping to think how much more dangerous a threat could be once educated. How if knowledge is power, and power can corrupt, then education is the fuel of grand destruction.

Boooom!

Solus' flesh pounded against the dome. Paul swung to the deafening force as it thundered in the hollow space. *Boooom! Boooom!* The sound reverberated and howled through the skylight. A sharp glitch on the far side of the room caught his peripheral. He rushed over. Solus was hitting the stone below Flora. The portrait twitched. Inch by inch slipping from its place with each thumping blow. It rattled disjointed, as Paul trembled. His throat got tight searching for a solution. Solus was willing to collapse the building with him in it if he didn't tell him what he wanted to know.

Paul pressed his body up against the mural, trying to push back the smooth piece of compact snow. The glistening ice gave no traction. His claws slipped and scraped with each knock. Six savage thrusts. The block dislodged, as a jailbreak of cold air rushed through the void. The shapes above collapsed to fill the void as the entire side unsteadily slumped. Paul stepped aside the loose portion as it slid to the center of the room. A pounding struck at the adjacent chunk.

Paul had to go, but couldn't do it. He couldn't forsake her. It was just a picture, but it was all he had. Watching her die twice was more than he could do.

"Tell me who it is!" Solus screamed through the wall. "Tell me! Who took my place! Tell me!" With every muffled verb came a vicious slam. A second block popped. The structure buckled.

"There's nothing to tell!" Paul yelled.

"Tell me!"

Boom!

"Please!

"Tell me!"

Boom!

"Don't do this! I'm begging you!" Paul cried as he touched his Flora. It shook and moved his flipper. His words drowned in the onslaught.

"Tell me!" Solus shouldered another block from the foundation. Flora's face sank misshapen, warped, uneven. Something warm and wet dripped down Paul's face.

"Please," Paul sniffed, "I love her."

The noise never stopped. Paul looked wearily into the night sky up at Pyxis. His home moaned, threatening to give way. He took a last evaluation of the structure. This was it. It had compensated all it could. It wouldn't survive another lost block. Perhaps this was for the better. Perhaps Solus was his alleviation. Someone to excuse him from a life he'd long stopped living. An undertaker, well overdue, come to collect a hollow shell.

One memory hovered in his thoughts. Embers, of a fear Paul could never force himself to forget. The overwhelming inability he felt when the sickness was coursing through his Flora. How he gazed, struck and powerless. He often wished he could rid his himself of this sorrow. That he could go back and play some part in the outcome. How he could've made it different. This time he had that choice. Now, some portion of power. This time she had a chance. *This time* he could save her. Paul frowned. Why was he risking the only thing he loved for someone he didn't? Why was he going through this for Pierre? Was it because he knew Flora's time had passed and he had to let go? Was it because he wanted to leave this world for hers? Was it because he felt it was death to give any name Solus thought linked with his banishment? Paul didn't know.

He surveyed what was left of his crippling sanctuary, and his mate. He gazed at the destruction, what had been done.

"What could Solus want this badly with Pierre?"

The words crept out above a whisper. Then something happened. It stopped. Impossible. He could barely hear himself think over the relentless clash let alone speak.

Solus panted heavily close on the other side. Then the breathing stopped. When life was gifted back to his limbs, Paul walked outside, and Solus was gone.

OISEAU THE KING CATCHER

Chapter 17

A breeze, heavy and hard, rushed over Pierre as the leader walked away. The formidable Chinstrap waddled waist deep in the water and ruminated on the horizon. The four assembled into position. Two diagonal rear-right, one slanted rear-left, and one in the middle. The form resembled a tilted "4." Pierre plugged into the spot posterior left and sighed.

Standing half a body in the ocean, the leader peered out into the tumbling waves. Looming in a meditative trance, the calm tide pushed him back and forth. "Xander, patience. Wranglers, make your noose furious. Stragglers, be ready for the burst."

The penguin across from Pierre shot a curious glance as if just noticing his presence. His belly hung low and he walked around it as he inched toward the surf.

The high noon sun scorched to its summit as six members squatted and leaned forward.

"Caaaatccchhhers!" the Sachem barked. "A-tta-que!"

The group splashed into the Atlantic surf without breaking form. Travelling at the butt of the brigade meant Pierre was a Straggler. A job he spent a great deal of time trying to get promoted from back home. With the expedition currently underway, the time for protest had passed.

Bubbling through the Epipelagic, an arrow of pointed jet streams riffled far from the coast. Each shadowed the leader's moves with split-second delay. Guided through tall sea forests and rainbow-shaded reefs. Swimming past clouds of trout, skipper, and silverfish. Pierre had budding doubts about the leader's keenness. Didn't he see them?

A melodic hum escalated as the camp gurgled past hordes of unsuspecting food. The catch shriveled slender as they puffed through obscure pockets of grey, blinded for a glimpse by the palls. The group dropped down south out of the last strange, underwater cloud, sinking into a circular gorge. A small canyon, and metropolis of nourishment. The fleet adjusted their angle, going from a flat line to an upward curve at full tilt. Pierre stirred to catch pace. Xander quickly moved level with the Sachem. They bolted through the surface, springing in twos, dripping wet bodies glistening for the sun.

"Wranglers! Fall out!" the Sachem shouted from above the others.

A pair of penguins in the second tier aborted ascent and sliced back into the ocean, splitting opposite directions once they hit the water. Xander and Sachem follow suit, falling like tears along the outsides of the rising Stragglers. Pierre and Puddles turn, and drop themselves back in.

All six were under. The two that fell in first started swirling a thunderous turbine around the biggest collection of quarry Pierre'd ever seen. Assuming the role of Master Spear, the leader swooned above the constricting snare while his partner drooped below. Taking their turns, they shot through the consolidated masses, picking off doubles and triples before returning to the surface and to loft it up for a flock of circling Albatross. Pierre stared though the watery window to the action above. One by one, blurry white birds filled their beaks and embarked for the colony.

The Wranglers bound the fish tight. Soon, they were too thick to pass through. Spears halted their attack as Pierre and counterpart hovered along the extremities. The Wranglers picked it up. Swirling and swirling faster and faster with mounting momentum. A globe of fish made small implosions, like a giant twitching orb. The equator shrunk. The prey crowded to the center until no more space was left at the core. They stopped. Pierre bobbed with the current.

A brilliant flash of scales bombed in every direction, bursting, like supernova in the bluish surroundings. Snaking in a stricken fury. Pierre steadied in the rushing stampede. He leaned and snapped, spun and shut, twirled and clamped. Snatching everything he could before tossing it to the couriers above. After ten trips he'd collared more than they had birds to carry. Whatever he launched up returned without interception.

On the other side of chaos, Puddles nibbled at whatever swam by. Managing to capture one for every twelve that bounced off his face. Twice he started toward the surface, stopped halfway, and ate what he caught.

Docking on the Cape, the crew wiggled themselves dry. When they looked for the tip of their sum, they kept looking. A mountain of wet, flopping bounty spilling out of the Reserve. Passers gawked at the earnings as the leader filed the tactical group in line. He opened his beak and closed it shut. He raised his flipper, then put it back at his side. He stood in front of Pierre. Kicked sand on his feet. Looked up. Squinted.

"You are obscure."

The Catcher at the opposite end waddled over to the clod, whispering numbers.

"Don't bother," the commander said, not pulling his focus. "You're wasting your time."

Xander slapped a corner, making that portion more wide than tall. "Looks can be deceiving," Xander said.

"To the easily deceived," the Sachem countered

"It may not be what we thought!" he squealed.

"Yes," the Sachem said spying Pierre like a dazzling gem.

"How do we know it's enough?"

"Because I've been counting catch since you were rattlin' around in your mama's gut. It's enough! Now Xander, please! Shut your Chub hole!" the commander snapped, giving Xander his full attention.

The other three shoved each other, and giggled. The commander peered quizzically with little regard for individual space.

Circling Pierre, the Sachem mumbled. He mumbled and circled, circled and mumbled until he made a small moat.

"Who the…What the…" He poked Pierre's flesh. "Lookin' like…" he slapped his belly "With the… I tell you what!" He rose up. "There's enough here to feed the colony, the albatross, and Puddles." A Macaroni slanted his head looking down the aisle. "Back in the line!"

The bird stood straight. Pierre took a breath.

"We're done," the Sachem snapped. "Disperse!"

The group was slow to move. They leaked out separately but ended up following Pierre. Walking steps behind like he was a creature they were compelled to examine. Pierre stopped to address the group. They looked into the distance. There was an awkward recess then one of them broke the silence.

"You hunt good," Puddles offered.

"I hunt good," Aria corrected, "what's the word for *this*?"

Xander pushed his way to the side of the small crowd. "Mediocre. Anyone can have one lucky day in the water."

Aria smirked. "How come you never got that lucky?"

"I have."

"Have not."

"Have too."

"No-you-have-not!" Puddles shook his flipper. "I would've remembered."

"He gathered the scraps I left behind," Xander scoffed.

Aria huffed. "Must've been a lot of scraps."

"Tasty scraps," Puddles added.

"Whatever! We can't go around getting excited because some penguin we don't know brought back a couple extra."

Aria pointed to the pyramid. "It's three times the daily catch, and would've been more if there were enough couriers."

"Sloppy tossing technique."

Puddles' face warped sour. "Ouuu ou ou! The ocean ain't the only thang salty."

Aria laughed. "Xander, I don't know how you see it, but this *is* a good thing."

Puddles turned to his partner. "Where'd you learn to do that?"

Pierre blinked, gazing down on Puddles as if he'd suddenly come to. "Um."

Xander pranced in front of the group. "Oh where'd you learn it," he mocked nasally. "It doesn't matter where he learned it! We can't trust him. That's what's important. Remember last time? We had a 'too-good-to-be-true' Catcher, and you saw how that turned out. He left. Gone. For chunks at a time and leaving us to starve. Remember? The small died. The healthy grew thin. So if he is everything you praise him to be, the only thing that really matters is how do we know he'll be there when we need him?"

A hush came upon the gathered. The Cape's lunch break was near, and every bird within an earshot drew to the congregation. Bundles of builders, healers, teachers, elderly, and albatross lifted a wondering stare.

Pierre's chest sunk a little. "He's right. I don't know how long I'll be here." Groans rumbled from the listeners. The crowd turned. "But I do know how it feels to go hungry. I know how it feels to share a fish between four, hoping it gets you through the night. I know how it feels for a colony to lose the ones they love when it didn't have to be so. And as long as I'm here, I will do everything in my power to make sure you never have to feel that way again."

They paused. Then the audience roared! The noise of a hundred seabirds echoed into air. Penguins trickled down toward the shore. Preservers came alarmed. In clusters they came and came until more than half were there.

The good news spread faster than gossip. As one citizen relayed to another and another, the details what was said was more warped and exaggerated. Quite quickly, the legend of Pierre's promise was greater than the promise itself. The mountainous pile amassed by the surf large enough for a bunch twice their size converted skeptics slow to believe the mysterious King penguin could make good on his promise. Upon hearing he'd gathered those on only the first round to sea, they fainted from glee. Without being said, it was unanimous. The hatching limitations were lifted. One egg per family was no longer applied. On the cusp of a mating season, the news could be no better.

Chapter 18

Patricia heard the news that night of her nephew's declaration and the Cape was more vibrant than ever. Caterwaul's sunset swim went longer, extending into the moonlight. Citizens were kinder, more patient. Builders spent extra time chiseling keepsakes and sculptures. They were happy and her home found new joy. The hope he restored was powerful and infectious, but she knew power goes both ways and so does hope.

Watching the splashes from her archway, Patricia walked across the beach to consult the only one who could assess what this truly meant for the colony. She arrived outside and sighed.

"And what you want?" an angry voice yelled from inside.

Patricia smiled, and ducked into the cave. That was as close to good evening as you were going to get from Sherri.

"So busy savin' and protectin' you ain't had time for Sherri. Treating me like some old crazy in a cave. Get over here." Sherri hugged Patricia hard and quick. The cave was dark with a topaz glow.

"I'm sorry Sherri. I've been—"

"You ain't been nothin'."

Patricia laughed.

"What you want?" She pronounced it 'wont'.

"I have to ask you a question."

Patricia paused. Sherri popped her eyes wide impatiently.

"How many eggs can this place hold?"

"We have exactly 146 seabirds on the cape including Pierre. Thirty families of three, 44 couples without egg, six widows and widowers; and six single folk. Assuming Pierre isn't spoken for."

"He isn't."

"Figured as much. Any male volunteering to watch eggs all day has a long life in front of 'em," she moved her beak quietly, "I can't say for sure, but we can hold a good amount. More than we're doing now I tell you that much."

"How many? If you had to guess."

"If I *had* to I'd say somewhere around fifty. In any one season."

"Okay," Patricia nodded, relaxing her shoulders a bit.

Sherri frowned, walking up under her. "Why? You plan on making me some eggs? You know I want them bad don't ya? I'm not getting any younger you know. You know, I'm not getting any younger."

"I do. Thanks for your help." Those sorts of questions didn't quite sting like they used to, but Patricia still wanted to run. "I promise I'll—"

"One last thing," Sherri suddenly wasn't loud anymore, and actually looked concerned. "You didn't have anything to do with that Banishment, did you?"

"Banishments happen on their own."

"Nothing happens on its own."

"Solus should have been sent away long before now."

"But he wasn't. 'Til now." There was a silence that lasted some while. "What did Pierre do back home?" Sherri asked.

"His job. What're you getting at Sherri?"

The short D.E.W. circled her. "There's danger in secrets, Patricia. We've never been a colony that keeps things from one another.

"I've always done what's best for Caterwaul."

"Nobody was calling for Solus' departure until you brought it up."

"Out of fear."

"Out of wisdom. Some things are good to fear. I didn't get this old by being brave. I know the fledglings here, I've raised every one of them until they were old enough for Academy and I've never known one like that one. He feeds on hate. If Solus thinks you had a part in this—"

"I don't care what Solus thinks!" The shout sounded through the cave. "I've been through a worse."

"Okay." Sherri said, stepping away softly, "Just be safe."

Patricia left the cave and the cool night's wind rushed to meet her. The sky was clear and though she tried she couldn't spot a cloud. The conversation took a turn for Solus, but that's not what took her mind. Sherri was right. There had been five mating seasons since she'd arrived in Caterwaul. Five opportunities and she expected nothing different from the sixth.

Chapter 19

"There are three divisions of Albatross," Aria explained, strolling the Cape on a sunny afternoon. "Messenger, Picker, Courier."

The commotion from earlier had cooled off. Or at least broken into smaller sub pockets, ripe with enthusiasm. Aria took Pierre from the madness, stealing him into a nook. The crowd hardly noticed. Once clear they spilled out toward the East. Putting a good distance between them and the crowd, they trotted into a stride and walked in the wet sand. Pierre was momentarily distracted by her eye contact.

She stuttered, "Umm, but our smallest division is the Messenger-Tross." She lifted her head. "They travel long spans through tortuous conditions remembering sequences of conversation. Whipping winds, thick rain, stinging hail, and scalding heat combat them at every passing. As you can imagine, few have the stamina, strength, and memory."

"I'd imagine very few have the will either," Pierre added.

"Quite the opposite. Messenger-Tross is a status of great prestige. Lady birds love the Ocean Runners. Most Albatross would like to be one, few get to."

Pierre nodded. It was the essence of why he wanted to become a Catcher back home. The respect of being a hunter, plus he could avoid the conflict of being a killer of his own kind.

"Next up is our Courier-Tross. Those are the ones that shadowed us on our expedition. As you've deduced, they collect our catch and bring it here to the Reserve. They have a filing-out system that assures there's always someone there intercept what we throw up. Today, you broke that system. They'll have to re-strategize."

Pierre almost apologized, but thought it a good problem to have.

"Excellent timing, swift swooping skills, and a muzzle like a trap. If Messenger-Tross are our marathon runners, they are the sprinters. A relay time of twelve taps of the claw to and from the hunting ground is needed to pass tryouts."

Pierre looked, imagining how far out to sea that could be from where they are. "You share food?"

"Yes, they get a portion of our take."

"What if they gobble the fish en route?"

Aria laughed, and slightly leaned forward. "We had that happen once. Every Catcher keeps an active count of how many fish they've collared, but for a while we couldn't figure out why the Reserve was coming up short. You can guess who we turned to first. But if that were happening in front of us all someone would've noticed. Considering the only other alternative, the Sachem met with the head of the Courier's order and devised a plan to smoke out the embezzler. In the midst of our catch, six triggerfish were thrown up. One per albatross. We'd been trained to identify what's dangerous in the ocean during Academy. If consumed, a triggerfish induces vomiting, muscle aches, dizziness, and hallucinations. To our surprise we found not one but two culprits dragging themselves in the sand when we got back. Regurgitating their portion, and hollering about dancing octopi. One was bold in his theft, claiming it was his right to get the get the first cut. He was Banished. The other recognized his error and begged for forgiveness. He was demoted, and removed from duty but allowed to stay. The remaining triggerfish were pulled from the Reserve before citizens were allowed to eat."

Pierre gawked, playing in still images some of what was just said. "That's a tough approach."

"Don't mess with the catch. We've got a lot riding on it." She paused, and then clapped. "Okay, Messenger, Courier, last one is Picker. Picker-Tross scavenge the wooded areas inland, sifting bushes and trees for nuts, fruits and leaves."

"For what?"

"Our alliance. If we want the Tree Dwellers to help us build our domes, there has to be a trade. Mainly they want fruit and leaves and not to have to do their own scavenging. Spend more time sleep and with the family, but some have developed more exotic tastes for things like Duckweed and Hydrilla. In which case we gather the foliage on our way back from the hunt."

"I see," Pierre said, overwhelmed. "That job seems relatively harmless. No threat of triggerfish, no capricious elements just rummage and gather."

She shook her head. "A popular misconception. Picker-Tross have to work the most harmful environment. The jungle. At any moment they could be mounted by a spotted leopard or stricken by a snake. To be an effective Picker they need three things—piercing vision, expert knowledge of the land, and a keen investigative mind. The faster you're in and out the better. There's no time to guess."

Where he grew up penguins only worked with other penguins. He had heard of Tree Dwellers in bedtime stories. What he thought was mostly a mixture of myth and meaning with very little world truth. His brother said he heard about them sometimes, from Quacks who had been on a guarded residency in South America. But imagined partnering with them on architecture.

"When not working," Aria continued, "or courting, they like to sit around and exaggerate tales of their heroics. Frank, is the worst one." The two subtly pulled alongside a huddle of webbed feet and yellow bills. All of them tucked and adjusted their feathers, getting still and folding them neatly.

"Listen," she said.

Pierre leaned in. Amidst the circle of large birds, one soft, high-pitched voice rose above the rest.

"I tell ya, there were at least 12 of 'em!" he worked the crowd, "teeth, sharp as fangs, claws, long as your head, and drooling. Drooling with the thirst for *murder*." There was some chatter, then the bird continued, "The hair on their fur stood like pointed thistles, highlighting the savage nature. I was backed against a tree, tall as the sky with a roof of branches barricading my only escape. There was nowhere to go, but onward," he pointed a wing, "into the belly of the beasts. A slow cloud passed above, shimmering a clear ray of daylight on the far side. That was my way out. I had to get there. But how? The creatures gnarled, their weighted steps cracking the dry branches. Movement all around, the smaller local residents retreating to their burrows and bushes. The monsters never even looked. That was the regular diet. They wanted albatross!" he hissed, dragging the esses in the last word. "At that moment, I steadied my trembling. I swallowed my rattling nerves. To get home…I was gonna have to fight my way out. Aaaaaiiiiiiiiiyyyy chop! I popped one on the head. *Hiiiiiiiya!* Dodged another to the left. *Tah!* I jumped. *Boof!* One knocked me down. I rolled into open space, looking up. They were closing. I kicked one in the chest, so hard I heard something pop!" Frank stopped, scanning the audience. "Brethren, it was war. Not for the faint of heart. I doubt many of you would've survived. It was just that raw!"

Aria tapped Pierre. "Frank here is referring about a pack of wild ocelots that roam the woodlands. And the reality is true enough, many birds have nearly been skinned by the vicious beasts, some didn't live to tell the story. However, you want to know what he really ran up against that day?"

Pierre slanted.

"Bunnies," she said with a punch.

"Bunnies?"

"Bunnies."

"How do you know?"

"Apparently, he grabbed a bushel of carrots, they hobbled curiously for a nibble, and he moistened himself running away."

Pierre hunched over laughing.

"His co-scout saw the whole thing. Said you could follow the drops all the way to Caterwaul!"

They both doubled over wheezing, trying to muzzle the sound.

"He's lying," she cackled, "and they know it."

Pierre raised his flippers. "So why listen?"

"I guess everyone likes to be entertained. But truthfully, there's no way any of them would stand a chance grounded in the jungle."

Aria took a while to reclaim her composure, standing up straight exhaling with a slow quiver. "Woo! Ahem, but yes, that's how we all coexist. Three groups, each providing services for the other in exchange for other services or food. We do something for them, they do something for us, everyone's happy."

Pierre and Aria continued their trek, approaching that narrow elevated entrance to Caterwaul. As they paused at its base, 10 furry beasts descended like dinosaurs down the ramp walking onto the beach. They moved in slow motion, pounding potholes into the sand. The smallest of them was at least three times Pierre's height, and the largest about five or six. Stepping left, Pierre stood next to his guide, awaiting instruction.

"Don't worry, they only want you if you taste like tree," she said. "They prefer plants over penguins."

Pierre was hoping his fear wasn't that obvious.

A grand mammal passed with hair a burnt orange and face flat as a rock. It stared straight down at Pierre with no expression, and then nodded. Pierre looked up, hesitant to move, then nodded furiously. Being small was unfamiliar, vulnerable, and absolutely frightening.

"What are we building today?" he asked, eyeing the giant figures tromping down the shore.

Aria looked off at the foreign twinkling objects floating on the distant sea. "Plugs."

Pierre was patient for an explanation.

After a thoughtful pause, she continued, "There's something out there. We're not sure what, but it wasn't there before, and it's hurting *everything* it touches."

Chapter 20

If Tiberius had known something was listening, he would have kept the message private. Stored away in the vault of his thoughts where it rightfully belonged. It wasn't uncommon for Messengers to practice their delivery aloud. In fact, it helped ensure memorization. No bird wanted to fly from Caterwaul to any destination, only to forget or misquote his or her verbal parcel. In the safe emptiness of Bouvet, Messenger-Tross stopped on their journey for rest and repetition. Some M.T.s had to travel as far as the corners of Australia, others, the northern tip of New Zealand or deep into the heart of Fiji. While Tiberius wasn't burdened with a voyage quite that far, he was the only one required to go into an active warzone. For many, the most important thing they were in risk of losing was their message. For Tiberius it was much more. The rules laid out by Patricia and Pierre's father were ever at the front of his consciousness, and he followed them with diligence.

Rule One: Enter at night. Well after the sun is down when the sky is at it's darkest.

Rule Two: Know your stars. If you get lost, navigate by constellation. Everyone's heard stories of the birds that lost their way. The ocean is a desert to the careless, and much of the world is far less civil than home. Before tighter restrictions of who was allowed into the craft, many turned around Messengers were doomed to wander the infinite Atlantic, while others found themselves in volatile places. The cover of darkness and guidance of stars are powerful allies.

Rule Three: Speak only in the old language. To veil the secrecy of content, the Falklands had their own dated dialect, or *Viejo Lenguaje*, completely dissimilar to Caterwaul's Langue de L'ancien. Pierre's mother, a native of The Falklands, knew the tongue very well, making her and her mate from Caterwaul a formidable linguistics team. Pierre's father received the message from Tiberius, passed it to his mother, and she would relay the information to his brother and other relatives. Nothing was more important than the message, and you could never be too safe.

Rule Four: Meet on high ground. Never risk ambush from above. The most important advantage a bird of the sky has over one of the sea is flight. If an albatross could be weighed down, he'd be tortured for what he knows and then tossed, sans vie, onto the doorsteps of the opposition.

Tiberius paced the glacial surface reviewing the fundamentals and mulling over what he was to deliver. The first part was mostly Patricia responding to comments and questions from Pierre's dad in the message prior. Next, she spent some time updating her brother on how well his son was adjusting. How he'd be proud of the penguin she saw him becoming—responsible, selfless, hard working. Then, a drastic change in mood as she exposed concerns. She saw the pit Pierre could be digging for himself, and how the Cape, for its own reasons, would let him. She said he didn't talk about it much, but she could see the deep hurt by their absence. She asked her brother if things were getting better. Despite being sure of the response, she felt it a duty to her nephew to ask.

Tiberius recited passages aloud rehearsing with seasoned prose. Enunciating his vowels and clicking his tongue on the hard consonants. Over his shoulder, he heard what sounded like claws tapping on ice. He turned. Nothing was there. Only the loud whistle of the wind and slow lapping of the sea. Tiberius took a calm panoramic scanning the land.

He never recited his message on Sud Afrique, for fear of a nosy eavesdropper who happened to know the dialect. In flight detracted too much focus from navigation. And never on The Falklands, for obvious reasons. Once a Messenger was seen as careless with his cargo, he was no longer trusted. Once untrusted, no one wants to work with him. No work, no contribution. No contribution, well...

Each corner of Caterwaul's Triangle Network had its own in-house whistleblowers. Publicly appointed penguins, tree dwellers, and albatross, who saw to the removal of the irresponsible and unproductive. Their job was simple—find the bad seed and remove it before it spoils the bunch. To maintain its share in the agreement, each group had to be vigilant in removing the leech. Those who drew on the collective produce without provisions of return. The colony learned the hard way, when one can eat and not work, others will want to know why they cannot do the same. Getting over is infectious, and sloth lay dormant in most every being. If that weed were to flourish, it would consume the colony. Reeling each species back to basic levels, having to relearn what nature taught them long ago: How to survive on their own.

Messaging was the only thing Tiberius knew how to do. He spent his whole life honing this craft, coming from a bloodline of Trans-Atlantic Runners. He learned to do it well, repetition the key. Preparation and practice, the two biggest factors to success and Bouvet was the only place a Courier could perfect their message with complete concentration. In complete solitude alone.

Or so he thought.

Chapter 21

Solus thought the elements were playing tricks. The sound of wings coming to a flutter echoed nearby was so loud he thought it a multitude. Had the festivities started already? He frowned. Too soon. Despite the perpetually arctic weather here, winter hadn't come yet. And the hustle and bustle of that monstrosity would have been hard to miss even from this part of the island. No, it must've only been one.

Solus rapped his claws against the ice. Birds of the sky never landed on Bouvet Island. Not to his knowledge. It was too cold, too remote, and their feathers could freeze over if they stayed any real period of time. They simply weren't built for the conditions, and since nothing was here, why risk it? Why come to this place? Yet there it was. That distinctive whoosh of descent, the rush of wind, the gentle tap of toes touching the tundra. The gust was so forceful it cleared the fog for a glimpse. Only one set of wings in all his travels were capable of whipping up such a roaring sound.

Solus calculated the odds and grinned. The stars favor the wronged. He walked carefully toward the noise. Through the climbing thicket of falling snow he saw a silhouette, marvelously familiar. He walked faster. The pale grey shadow turned in his direction. He took a few sharp sprints and slipped into the sea. Not pausing to let the water settle, he moved closer and closer through the liquid. A few feet away, his head barely above surface, he hid below the small shelf of ice, no more than a foot tall that separated land from sea. Mumbles turned into words. Solus hovered, leaned in, and listened intently.

Chapter 22

"We've seen similar symptoms in a cartographer who used to work here," Aria continued while Pierre gazed at the large ships far off shore. She pointed. "Dead fish, dead plants. Anything too close for too long was faded without color."

Pierre crumpled his brow. "Do we know what it looks like?"

"Thick liquid, darker than the rest. Medics have been making brief trips to the site. They found that there are holes in the ocean skimmer. Puncture marks where the surrounding water took a smoky grey color. They suffered lightheadedness, returning disoriented even from the shorter trips. Whatever's leaking from those holes, it's dangerous. And we think it's spreading. The range," she did a slow wide circle with her flipper "is wider than it used to be and more concentrated. It's meeting us further out. Which by all assessments means it's coming closer. "

"You sure the plugs will work?" Pierre's uncertainty sounded like pessimism, though not intended that way.

She looked up. "It's possible. There's speculation that if we don't obstruct the flow, Caterwaul won't last through the season."

Pierre looked out at the strange vessels and recalled the faint hum he'd heard during their expedition. It sounded like a distant Blue Whale, calling her calf to come home. But this information shed new light. The objects on the horizon were already the second of two things Pierre never saw before today. He thought of the Cape, and it's impenetrable calm to know something so lethal was so close and not be in a stupor. "If it doesn't work, what's everyone going to do?"

"Nothing," she replied, all too placid. "Most don't know. Just the Catchers who have to go far out there, two medics on analysis, and the pair of Builders designing the plugs."

"They don't know?"

"It's far enough off shore, and we're taking measures to stop it. What can they do, besides panic?"

"They should know."

"And take the only peace they've had since The Lack? It's taken us a long time to feel at ease again. In one day you've given them hope. To believe they can have the family they've wanted and the life they remember. Do you want to throw that away for a hypothetical?"

Pierre's conscience burned with the dilemma. He was new. Just walked through the twin mountains a night before and it wasn't in a place to incite psychological pandemic about something he didn't fully understand. But secrets had a dark past with him, and in his past, when it comes to light, secrets only benefit the secretive.

Chapter 23

"Vous serez fier de le pingouin votre jeune est devenu," quoted the giant bird, clearing his throat, adjusting his diction. *"Hier, il était nouveau et venait d'arriver. Maintenant, après une seule chasse, les citoyens sont prêts à le traiter comme il possède l'endroit!"* Tiberius strained to deliver in the same enthusiasm as Patricia. *"Ils ont bien mangé aujourd'hui, à son crédit. L'Attrape-Roi est ce que certains ont commencé à l'appeler en privé. Probablement parce qu'ils ne savent pas son prénom. Mais à sa vieille tante, il est encore tout simplement Pierre."* He paused for the part that gave a problem. *"L'Attrape-Roi. L'Attrape-Roi,"* he repeated, with alternating fluctuation. High, then low. He paced, playing with the verbiage, trying to find the most significant way. This was the climax. It needed to be delivered as such.

He spread his wings, a massive twelve and a half-feet of reddish-brown feather, flapping as he did every so often to keep cold pellets of snow from settling and sticking patches together. Ridding them of the moisture, he checked his surroundings. Squinting ineffectively into the bright white cloak. Water and ice around, mountains and snow above. Empty. Wiggling his neck, he returned to his monologue and switched dialects. Working a bit in his natural language always helped deliver the proper pitch, earning praise from his recipients. The elocutionist reformed the phrase again and again in his speech:

"*L'Attrape-Roi. L'Attrape-Roi,*" he said, "The Catcher of Kings?" No. "L'Attrape-Roi. The King's Catcher?" Doesn't make sense. "The Catcher King?" Something still doesn't translate right. What is it? He was vexed. Tiberius tried to place the words that caught him in a snare into proper context. What he knew about Pierre, about the message, about the cape. Rays of clarity burned through mental fog. "The King Catcher. *L'Attrape-Roi.* Pierre, the King Catcher." Tiberius huffed his chest, impressed with the fruit of his work. A good Messenger never simply regurgitated his parcel like a father feeding his young. The magic was in capturing the essence of what it is to be delivered, and giving it in a way that made the audience feel they were at the feet of their loved ones. Not theatrics, sincerity. Not showmanship, accuracy. To care enough to present a message how they'd want to hear it, and to always be sensitive to the underlying truth. You are all they have. You are all that connects them.

As Tiberius primed himself for a last round before taking off, a stir swirled in the liquid nearby. He turned to a sound he could only describe as unnatural. Healthily paranoid, he etched forward fluttering his wings once more to shake loose the snow. He propped them half-open. Leaning his neck over the edge, he stared into the dark blue. What he found warmed him with caution and intrigue. A red light gazing up from under the surface, making a wavering circular impression atop the water. What was this?

Go. Curiosity wasn't worth it. But protocol demanded he assure the message wasn't compromised. That he wasn't being spied on. We already talked about what happens to those who become untrusted. If the Falklands learned of this place as a hub for Messengers it didn't take much imagination to know they'd send a scout to syphon intelligence. The control of information was critical and those who intercepted it earned precious leverage. Tiberius had to be sure. His name depended on it. The glow was puzzling. His mind went to a trio of places. An underwater volcano? He'd heard of them, but up this far? The wind? He'd never heard it like that. Maybe something fell prey, which would explain the sound and color but not the glow?

He stretched his beak out far to get a better look. His body weight leaned back not to tip over. The faint swirl of movement. Tiberius put his ear to the water to see if he could identify the size of what he unfortunately presumed to be an animal. If it sounded anything bigger than a penguin he was out of here. Tiberius took shallow breaths and listened. Silence. He swiveled his head to face the water and to his horror the fiery blaze was getting smaller at a rapid pace. The haze grew more concentrated, more near. It came to focus. *It was...a face.*

Wide jaws burst through the surface clamping him round the throat. It twisted, jerked, and snatched him asunder. Something hung heavy on his neck as Tiberius was ripped through the icy water. Pain spiked in every nerve. Trapped in a red flurry of red bubbles, the luminous murk clouded his vision. The grip was tethered to his throat. Tiberius lashed wildly, hoping his talons would hit flesh. After four frantic strikes his claws pushed into something plush and blubbery. The wringing clasp quickly released. Flapping his wings trying to fly to the surface, Tiberius broke through to the world above and vacuumed a feast of air into shocked lungs. Dragging back up onto the ice, he slid his dripping body across the cold frigid ground, pushing away from the edge. Pacing backward, he stood and tried to shake himself dry, but the salty liquid was soaked to the bone. He jumped, and the takeoff failed with a damp hard smack, his clumped feathers more like oars than sails. He tried again. This time managing to get a foot or two north before falling back to Earth. He shook briskly, flinging beads of water. Flapping his wings, he tried again. More lift, but not nearly enough for sustained flight. Anchored, he couldn't sustain flight. The threat of dropping into the ocean after takeoff would render him worse than before. A wounded victim for any nearby with a taste for albatross. If he didn't shed the water in his wings before the arctic turned it to ice, he'd never escape alive.

A plateau about six feet tall was in the distance. He needed a safe place to dry off. No sooner than he saw the elevated haven, a black and white blur torpedoed out of the ocean with such force it looked as though the very Atlantic had spit him out. Sliding on a slick stretch of ice, it rose, scarred and tall. Tiberius recognized the bird and stepped back. He took a step back, then another and another. He thought for sure that the last time he'd seen him was the last time he ever would. Yet, standing in front of him, glistening in the glum grey was the horrid outcast. The one he'd watched dumped on this island and abandoned without a thought. Ooze trickled from three fresh puncture wounds on his left chest, the result of Tiberius' attack.

Across the tundra, a few yards apart, Tiberius' glare trailed up to the crimson pockets of light burrowed in Solus' head. Snow fell diagonally between them in a steady flush. Solus looked in no rush to pursue. *This was planned.* The albatross grew more alarmed. He could not fly for his life and his adversary was counting on it. The drip of Tiberius' feathers kept him constantly surrounded by water.

Snnnap! Snnnap! Echoes pierced through vacant landscape. The clap of Solus' beak sounded like a thick branch breaking and a sudden shudder caused Tiberius to slip. As he lay there fumbling and wet, Tiberius felt something climb up inside of him.

Something he had only heard of. Deep and immediate dread. Not a fear that comes with going in and out of the warring Falklands, one that subsided and became more diluted with each safe passage. This was present. Materialized and dark. Mounting and specific.

Tiberius kicked with his trembling webbed feet, his efforts doing little to slide him along the ice. His short talons couldn't grip the tundra as they scratched and scraped with no result. As he got up, they provided a momentary stasis before slipping from under him again.

He braced for the hunt, but Solus lurked with a patient stalk as if having nowhere else to be or go. Tiberius mind was in a race, done piecing together the 'what' and the 'who' and now wrapped in the 'why.' Why had he been dragged under the cold stinging sea? Why he was badly bruised around the neck and standing on a deserted island with Solus? Why was he doing this? Tiberius hoped Solus didn't remember him standing around at his Banishment. If he did...the thought rushed and the albatross couldn't locate bravery. Solus was here because they put him here. Politics of who was at fault meant less to Solus than it did to him. The Fiordland was marooned in this place convinced of a notion that no doubt festered in his mind. And here today, the albatross was the embodiment of an entire Cape's decision. Falling again, Tiberius huffed. There was no reasoning, or convincing, just the reality of the wronged and the surety of revenge.

OISEAU THE KING CATCHER

Chapter 24

Solus moved patiently upon the cowering albatross. He thought of his successes. What he did to Paul. The rumble of professor Jaunty's house crumbling in the distance and quaked the frontier. A thing that badly damaged was bound to break. He would join Flora after all. Solus steeped with pleasure shoveling the thought from his mind, focusing on the now. The good albatross was in his presence, and deserved his full attention. After all, it was time for an extraction. Paul, in a stuttering panic forfeited half a treasure, and the rest was sunken inside the messenger.

The island's dismal visibility was worsening drastically through the shield of falling snow. Earlier, Solus could only see eight or nine steps in front of him. Now, that eight or nine had easily dropped to four or five. The riot of white was blinding, and Solus kept within constant view of his prisoner. Creeping forward as he slid. The messenger was weighted to the cold ice desperately trying to push back on a wet webbed foot.

Solus was close, casting his shadow on the sad bird. Tiberius swung. The drenched appendages making lethargic attacks. He swung again. Solus calmly leaned back both times watching wings sail by in slow motion. Flipping over and hopping to his feet, Tiberius fluttered, managing to hover three feet. He lunged. Solus dropped one foot back and turned sideways. Tiberius zipped past and Solus charged. Clapping his wings out front, the albatross pivoted in time to channel a powerful burst of wind into Solus' chest. The wings were no good for flying, but they commanded enough force to drive Solus back on the slick surface.

Solus squinted, struggling through the onslaught. Water flicked from the bird's feathers with every thrust. Solus growled, anchoring his claws into the ice, staggering forward. Tiberius flapped harder, in strong wide strokes. Solus pressed on steadily putting one foot in front the other. The gap was shriveling. Solus was close, nearly touching his feather. Tiberius shifted his wings, dropping them for flight. The resistance stopped. Solus shot toward his prey.

Four quick kicks and Solus dropped flat on his stomach. The sound of his body rushing on the ice was like running water. Tiberius shakily tilted and lifted. Flitting further from Bouvet. The Fiordland clenched tighter. Tiberius leveled out, giving a hard push.

Solus leapt. A cloud passed and unobstructed sunlight showered through with the snow. Solus felt a hard knob of bone in his beak. With a turn, Solus slammed his body to the surface with a loud crack.

The bird rolled over and kicked. Annoyed, Solus swatted it away. He stood over Tiberius and hammered his ribcage until he heard something split. The body went limp. A shallow breath faintly moved the shell. His physical will to resist drained. Tiberius winced, curling into a ball before Solus' foot came sliding up his neck pinning him flat to the cold hard ice.

"I'm no fool," Solus said, "I know exactly how the Cape works. For one to come, one must go. Only room for so many stomachs, and I was your chosen sacrifice. I should have been immune, for what I provided. After all, how could Caterwaul survive without its greatest Catcher? How could it get along without the beak that feeds it? Given my current position, I've had time to think and it didn't take long. There was only one way, really. You found a replacement. Someone who could do my job, who could carry my load, at that point I became expendable. Something to be tossed out and driven into the wild. Pierre the King Catcher!" he said with sarcastic regality. "As you so affectionately call him. Summoned all the way from the Falklands so you could get rid of little old me. Ouch. But you're in the business of telling things, so now tell me something." Solus leaned in and whispered, "Tell me how I can meet him?"

Tiberius said nothing. Solus bent his slunk frame erect, contorted his neck bending it back bringing it around in a full circle before whipping it down.

"There are two options," Solus said, "And I think you're smart enough to know what they are." Solus tightened his grip. The albatross squirmed under the weight, twisting, pleading for an inch. Solus jammed his outside claws into the ice on the sides of Tiberius' neck creating a jagged barricade around his throat.

"Wiggling would be ill-advised. Tell me what I want to know and please don't lie like my mother."

Solus' middle talon slowly descended on Tiberius' trachea, sifting through a thin layer of feathers, prickling against the bare skin. Solus wanted the bird to know the price of refusal. Tiberius took short sharp breaths. Solus' eyes flickered with a wild blaze like staring into a bright gem as he pressed his weight. The skin sunk in the section of the nail, and more inhale and it was ready to give.

Chapter 25

It didn't take a builder to see the structure was unfit for living. The Adam of Caterwaulian architecture, once perfectly arched, was now a ruin lopsided and slumped. Paul looked around, wondering what would be its demise, as a breeze pushed a loose rhombus to the inner chamber, dropping the blocks in a thunder. He left Flora, and he wasn't proud of it, had he been within they would've shared the same fate. Gawking at fresh rubble, he was compelled to weep but couldn't. History impotent to repeat itself no matter how hard it tried. He'd cried that cry. Years ago and many days since. He looked up into the snowy overcast imagining Pyxis shining bright in a decorated sky. His chest rose and fell with the flower-scented air that occasionally visited the tundra and Paul was warm.

He basked a moment before the smile fell. By whispering his name he threw Pierre into danger. The encounter made him panic, the panic made his thoughts rush, the thoughts turned to words. Paul felt shame. Shame in how he'd been, shame in what he wanted, in what he didn't want—anymore. The Celestial Nest, an end for all, should be a destination for none. Paul acknowledged that his yearning for the life after was a temporary thirst. Loss created a pit deep as a trench, and depression turned his mind to thinking nothing was left. It was the easiest way to deal with a life that had become too hard to live. But when faced with an escape, a free ride, a blind ferryman that required no token, he couldn't take the trip.

There was something he had to do now. Pierre would suffer a much worse fate at Solus' mercy than that of a leopard seal. Because Paul knew the most vicious predators of all are your own kind. In his portly glory Paul found himself once again tasked to save a king penguin twice his size. Heading east down the isle, following a trail of dim webbed footprints fading in the falling snow, Paul Jaunty lowered his head and entered the storm.

Walking cautiously, he pursued Solus. Perpetual grey overcast made it impossible to tell how long he had been on the hunt. At times, he heard shuffling nearby and backed away. Others, when the faint rustlings were afar and he rushed quietly, like quick whispers, to close the distance. Being shrouded by the snowstorm, Paul followed noises and tracks. Rushes of nervousness tempted him to attack, get it over with, be done, none of this torturous teeming anxiety. But such actions would serve the dual function of both committing suicide and accomplishing nothing. At this point, Paul wanted neither. What the old professor really wanted, nay, needed, was information. The plan brewing to remove Pierre. The occasional splutter of spiteful thoughts echoed from Solus' concerning Caterwaul. Talks about his Banishment and overall discontent. Paul kept sly attention to the grumbling, analyzing best he could, knowing a soul alone speaks the truth.

The weather transformed Bouvet to a labyrinth. Rapidly descending snow now poured into the footprints covering tracks in short time. Paul had to adjust his speed with the climate change. Falling too far behind now would assure he'd get lost. Trailing marks fresher and fresher in the ground, Paul was close enough to hear the solid bird's steps crush soft ground. Paul stopped. Exhaling with a quiver he stepped, lightly as his body allowed. His heart thumped in palpitations. The prints cut off at the water's edge. Paul leaned over pondering if Solus had left Bouvet with the name. If he had he gone back, in denial, like a pup pushing for an udder when there aren't enough? Forcing, looking to be loved by something with none to spare. Paul looked out across the waves. Maybe it was the only thing that ever loved him. No matter how short, shallow, or circumstantial. For his gift, whether they wanted to or not, he was loved. Now, without that purpose, he was exactly what his life told him he was. Worthless. Abandoned by a father, the smallest concern of a mother, who focused more on the one that wasn't there than the one who was, and now cast from his only home to make room for a better offspring. A nobler son.

Standing at its edge, the ocean slapped against the island. Going in would put him at a great disadvantage, even more than on land. He turned and looked into the slanting snow. Solus was absent, at least from Paul. But despite the possibilities of travel, and how bad he wanted to return home, Solus had nowhere to go. Every bit of his primal strength was nothing to a hoard of Preservers. His name and face were notorious. There was no sandy expanse, no corner, crevice, or crèche for him to hide in or live amongst.

A crack, like the loud split of ice, sounded in the mist. Paul rushed in the direction. Through a haze, he saw something misshapen. One body, no, two. Solus was standing, but something was under him. Approaching the edge of his cover, Paul saw it was a large bird pressed tightly under foot. Instincts urged Paul to charge, knowing what Solus would do. But bits of the conversation confused him. Was this a struggle between enemies or a disagreement between partners? How could he be sure? He decided to learn. The pinned bird sounded calm, like water in a brook. Certainly much more than Paul himself was earlier that afternoon under a similar situation. Something was wrong.

Relentless howls and noisy thrushes of air made it impossible to take in every word. Sometimes, Paul would get whole sentences and others, garbled bits. The head of the albatross turned his direction.

OISEAU THE KING CATCHER

Chapter 26

His prey didn't move. It couldn't. It didn't blink because it dared not to. Despite a valiant façade, Solus could still see the fear seeping from every unchecked motion, every dash of the eye, every wring of the torso, every hastened breath, and hard swallow betrayed the bird's cool exterior, and yet the albatross seemed determined not to obey.

"Mmm yes, the vow of secrecy," Solus muttered after a pause. "Rules of a bunch of penguins that are more important than your own life. Tell me something, do you even know what you'd be dying for?"

Tiberius stared up.

Solus stretched his neck forward and widened his eyes. "I'd question any rule you have no say in making, but must follow to the death. Does that make you a partner, Tiberius? Hmm? Would they die for *your* secrets?"

"I've taken a pledge," the albatross gritted.

Solus held his nail firm at the flesh's breaking point. "You've yielded to an obligation and you think this makes you equal?" He paused. "You're a tool, Messenger, nothing more. A tool to build with. If it breaks, they'll get another tool."

"I am no tool."

Solus tilted his head and tucked a slight grin. "Because you choose your own meal at the Reserve, you believe you are free?"

"I am free."

"And that's why you're not. They don't need to trap your body when they have your mind. You have a powerful wingspan that could travel the world, and yet only go where they tell you."

"I didn't have to be a Messenger."

"But you had to be something. An option isn't the same as a choice. You had to fit in one of their slots. What would you really be doing if you had your say? Flying chatter between relatives? See that's what freedom truly is, your own course, Tiberius, without restriction."

"*I am free.*"

"You're poisoned. Even now the notion of nobility has oiled the clear waters of your thinking. That's why you deny, that's why you push, but I implore you, don't be courageous be intelligent. What gets you out of here alive? Wouldn't *they* want you alive?"

In that moment, Tiberius' eyes strained to the left, far as the sockets would allow, he quickly turned his head and dragged Solus' long talon across his throat. It nicked the skin and blood seeped slowly to the surface.

"Look at me!" Solus lost his even tone. Tiberius looked. Solus pressed the claw deeper. "It's just us. I made sure of that, but I will ki...." Solus took a moment to reseat his poise, and drew a long breath. "Be selfish, as they have. Think what you have to lose! That one you'll never meet, the young you'll never have. You're worth that much, right? Do you have to give *all* that up…for them?" Tiberius sunk slightly. "They ask so much but what do they risk? What do they risk, for *you*?" Solus paused to let perspective linger.

The albatross was computing. He was ready.

Solus spoke calmly, as if a longtime friend. A contrast to the reality of the talon he had digging at his throat. "All I want is information. Does he take long swims, go to secluded areas, does he sleep by himself. Everyone has private time."

The sharp nail was digging into the slightly cut flesh.

"Self-preservation can be so rewarding."

Solus' foot pushed deeper into his neck. Air was trapped at the bottom of his throat, obstructing his ability to breathe. The albatross had a decision. Live a traitor or die loyal. His chest convulsed, red roots crept from the corner of his eyes. Tiberius slowly lifted his gaze, and split his beak.

Chapter 27

Paul lunged from the white, ramming Solus in the stomach and knocking him out of sight.

"What did you tell him?" Paul demanded. Focusing where Solus slid off.

Paul nudged Tiberius to his feet. No response. Paul glanced at the bird, red dripping down the radiant white breastplate. Tiberius hung a blank gaze. He looked at Paul, then the ground. Paul was furious, but in no position to gripe. He too had given Solus what he asked for in a different way.

"Can you fly?" Paul's attention dashed between the albatross and the steady thicket of snow.

Tiberius jerkily spread his wings to full mass.

"Good. Go back. Tell Pierre he's in danger."

The bird paused. Paul guessed hesitance from his trauma.

"Albatross! It's not your fault. But if you don't warn Pierre, whatever happens next will be. Now get out of here Flock!"

Tiberius crouched, exploding wildly into the falling snow. He looked down. Solus and Paul were locked in a vicious fury. Sharp darting pains shot to the tips of his wings, causing sudden dips and lulls. He wasn't sure if he could make the short flight, or if he'd fall into the Atlantic, hurt and vulnerable for anything circling with teeth. Leaving the island that should've been his grave, Tiberius felt more ashamed by what he thought than said. A seed had impregnated his mind and he couldn't turn his thoughts from one question: *Am I free?*

Chapter 28

Paul was on the run. He managed to wrestle away into the fog, but Solus hunted him. Glares of red flickered in his peripheral, as this big island felt like a very small room. Staggering, with cuts along his side from the tussle. He had to return to Caterwaul. He had to warn Pierre. Paul eased into the water. The blood from his wounds seeped out into the sea. A stir churned below. He hopped out. Footsteps rushed his way. Paul lay down to quiet the sound of water dripping on ice. A red haze like a light tower swept the area. Paul cringed into a circle, squinting hard.

"Come out and I will end this for you. No more being afraid. No more living in pain. You can be happy. I'll help." Footsteps clicked between the words as his overgrown claws tapped the ground. "You've lived a full life. One to be proud of. Don't spend the end of it like this. Have control of it. Come and take what you deserve. You deserve more than what this life has left to give you."

Stuck between a vengeful Solus and a hungry ocean, Paul searched through the fog. One of them must go.

Chapter 29

Fifty rises of the sun had passed. Pierre looked around at Caterwaul's new faces with growing concern. It was now the climax of the mating season and the colony had taken full advantage of his promise. In little over seven weeks Pierre had become a local icon. Wee-Waddlers, Tee-Waddlers and even some adults spent their lunches standing at the shore guessing how many he would collar. A trio of small regulars escalating in height always had the prime position. Pierre overheard their conversation recycle without waver.

"How many do you think he'll catch today?" one would say.

"If I had to guess, I'd say seven-hundred. That's sounds right. And you?" responded the other.

"Seven-hundred and fifty."

They both turned to the smallest one. "What about you Bella?"

A beautiful fairy penguin with soggy cheeks and bright blue eyes looked up. "Four," she said, absolutely sure, before returning to the mound of sand in front of her.

They declared predictions, and without fail, the total would never disappoint.

It was nothing he ever asked for, royalty, and honestly nothing he ever desired. The purpose felt good, to know while detained, he could build a better life for someone. But the admiration, while amusing, but often felt misplaced. The massive number of fish made them easy to catch. He was used to working with few. This wasn't something he earned, but more so just fell into. For that, he wanted no glory, no homage. Still, if the masses treat you like royalty long enough, fending off hubris becomes an occupation. Oh, how it felt to be young, and good at something.

Pierre was never special or important to anyone not blood-related. But for now, at least for now, marooned on this stretch of sand he was truly a King. The glitz and benefits were fully adorned. Preservers took him on private tours of beautiful and exclusive parts of the Cape, he was asked to skip the line at the Reserve, and Builders spent extra shifts creating a lavish chamber. Perhaps it was innocent, possibly courtship, maybe it was kindness, or pure sheer persuasion but either way it made limbo a little better.

After another exhausting day, Pierre reclined in the comfort of his favorite lookout. A high hill, taller and more inaccessible than the rest, where he watched the Cape play. Every day without fail after the work was done they got together to do what seabirds love to do best, be at sea. Pierre admired that about this place. He gazed over splashes in the sunset and exhaled to sleep.

Chapter 30

Heavy sounds of panting and sloshing ascended quickly, shaking Pierre from his rest. A form that he had grown close to during his time there became visible over the apex.

Pierre sat up to the huffs of a bird sounding like air was tough to catch. He wasn't sure why she paid him a visit but a probing question hung for which he needed an answer. While Aria sought to calm her breathing Pierre took the lead.

"Since we're here, alone, can I ask you something?"

Aria straightened to form still chasing wind. "You just did."

They both snickered, mocking the Sachem. One of them asked to ask something every day just to hear the recycled wit.

Their laughs fell into a chuckle and then a smile before Pierre continued, "It never seemed right to ask in front of a crowd. Being Catchers we always seem to be in one. What's The Lack?"

Pierre had heard the phrase often whispered in huddles when he first arrived. A certain reverence or hesitance accompanied it, but over time, he heard it less and less. Her eyes met his in a hurry.

Her gaze, stern and alarming before dropping into something soft and unsettled.

"I'm sorry, I…" He stood.

"No, you deserve to know." She took a breath and walked to the edge. "Not so long ago, we had kind of a tough time. There was a drought, so to speak. The fish were there, but we couldn't harness enough to match the number growing of mouths. We started taking turns, half of us ate every other sunset to make sure there was enough. That turned into every two sunsets, then three. Soon, chaos broke as penguins stormed the Reserve, taking what they could for them and their family. More Preservers were charged with governing the rations, which lead to less decreased border patrol, fewer predator scouts, and a drop in civil policing. Our Cape cracked into anarchy, and many died of starvation. Some were attacked by outsiders, others beaten in the night for what they had."

Pierre crept next to her.

"Worst part was, we couldn't do anything. There was no way to fix it. Which, honestly, is why I'm here. The Cape is getting bigger Pierre. And I know you won't be here forever." She paused, her gaze fell to the floor. "If we could barely support the citizens we had when you arrived, what are we going to do with a group twice its size once you leave?" She watched the Cape at play. "We're not prepared for this."

Aria turned to Pierre. "If that's still the case come your departure, it'll be The Lack all over again."

Pierre followed the logic, but felt something stir.

"Aria, if I get a chance to go home, I'm going to take it."

"I know. I would never ask you not to, but it's bigger than that. You won't live forever, and everyone down there is either too blissful or blind to realize what I did the other day. No matter how it happens or when, I…we *will* be without Pierre Oiseau one day, and there is nothing I can do to stop it."

Pierre charged to rebut but couldn't find the words. He never pondered life after his own. And before Aria shoved it in his face like Paul Jaunty's Chub, he never had to.

"Our system is flawed," she continued. "We can't rest our future on the slim shoulders of some penguin passing in the night."

"They're not that slim," Pierre grumbled, checking.

"I'm serious. We need a plan. We need more. Either way you look at it, you're not enough."

Pierre looked out over the citizens, peering down upon them from his sandy tower. He tried to count the bunch but lost his number.

"What should we do?"

Chapter 31

Pierre's father used to tell him fair is a word for the weather, and that adults dealt in reality, which often never is. Aria was bold and presumptuous, commanding he take responsibility for their future. After the talk, one ringing sentiment hummed in his mind: I don't belong to them. I am not theirs to delegate. Why was this mine? He asked again and again. But in silence, there was no room for reasoning or forum for righteous cause. The true possibility was frightening. New little faces sprinkled the shore, hard to ignore and harder to keep track of. There, whenever he would come striding out of the frothy Atlantic to greet him in an onslaught questions. Clearly the Cape wasn't at capacity anymore, it was above it. Despite stretches of open real estate, the colony had clearly bred beyond their means.

When he got here Pierre just wanted to do what he thought he could. Be a boost to their hunting system and help rebuild some of what was lost. He didn't care about the burden. If everyone was full then the Catchers did their part. But Aria made him realize the

Pierre-centric system he created, and what would come of it once he was removed. The thought shook him.

Forced to act, Pierre worked twice a day with the crew of Catchers post-expedition to improve their hunting skills. Mending minds with the Sachem, they came to a mixture of what the seasoned Chinstrap honed at home and the immigrant King developed on the islands. The result was the Amalgam, a six-point regiment to sharpen every approach.

One: Weight Resistance. Small rocks were wrapped to the penguin as it swam distance. Added bulk and forced change of direction designed to enhance strength of stroke. Common knowledge said a penguin could get to the hunting zone in 240 taps of the claw. Their goal was 180. Fatigue was a major factor that accounted for the drop in production on rounds three and four of the hunt. They had to be more effective, for longer periods of time. Stamina and power were the root.

Two: BCC or Blind-Catch Cultivation. Lead out to a scattered part of the sea, a Catcher was spun a dozen times. The disorienting haze acted to disrupt the equilibrium and provide a mild form of vertigo. Deciphering real prey from fuzzy projections conjured by their swirling mind before dinner got away. Catching dizzy served to optimize focus, and heighten reliance on other senses. As the fish move the water around you, you feel it ripple against your feather, wave over your body. Through submerged sonics you know all you need to know. Many chased blurry hallucinations through the deep dark blue, thinking they'd gotten their prey, only to snap down and have it dissipate. *Vision is the crutch.* Your eyes may've told a woozy lie. Sometimes you must feel your way through. A lesson Pierre learned well.

Three: Vortex Sync. Timing is everything. Especially in a group. Assuring the Wranglers were of equal distance and equal speed when circling fish was paramount. For Stragglers to make the most out of that brief, short, panicked burst they had to gauge exactly when it was going to occur. When left guessing, reactions were sloppy and wasteful. They practiced their lasso relentlessly, working to be on a string every time. As a more functional unit, they could catch more fish with less energy.

Four: Agility Trials. The live coral reef extending from the Cape was a beautiful maze of pockets, tunnels, and bends providing an ideal obstacle course for reactionary training. They'll never try to outswim you in a straight line. For fish, even their base instinct quickly tells them that isn't going to work, instead, they make cuts. Frantic and irrational hoping to do with quickness what they could not do with speed. The group wove through the colorful craters, rolling, dropping, and sprinting through gaps in the growth. For what they sought to hunt, in the psyche of their sustenance there was no pattern, process, or thought. Which made agility all the more valuable.

Five: The Chase & Escape. You won't always be the only one looking for a meal. In the event you find yourself on the fish's end you'll have to know what to do. The Sachem orchestrated simulated pursuits, at random during every day catches with the help of off-duty Preservers. Some days, even he didn't know when they were going to ambush. An enemy has no schedule. Thus, Sachem and Pierre thought it best they be as prepared as the rest of them. The exercise was designed for one thing—to practice calculated responses throughout rushing adrenaline. Pierre reminded the more dedicated of the group that if you have to choose between life and lunch choose the former. For Puddles, this was hard. Aria too.

The last provision was an individual stipulation Pierre demanded as the only trade for his devotion. Pierre still thought it unsafe that citizens outside the circle had no clue of the impending danger created by the monsters. But also spreading hearsay and inciting an S.O.E. wasn't his call to make. However, with Catchers going out there every day they at least had to be able to identify what it looked like. Ill hunters helped no one, and dead ones even less. The areas saturated with the grey became known as The Still. Just as reported, everything within the scope was withered and motionless. Plants lost vibrant green, animals suffered worse. The coral in that section was an ash-white skeleton brittle and mute. It was a graveyard and nothing was exempt. Medics noted the tint of the toxin had been at a stasis since the plugs were applied. No darker no lighter from the day Pierre first met the Tree Dwellers. That episode was a triumph for the enthusiastic eight in the know – three catchers, two builders, a pair of medics, and Patricia.

As the clumps of days rolled by and stars hid in the presence of a brighter light, clashing into the time of procreation, Pierre reminded the group to focus on what they could control. Telling the crew that the progress being made was really exciting, and that one day, they'd be better than him. The truth was far less jubilant. Pierre had schemed and thought, planned and plotted, prepared, tinkered and taught. Came early, stayed late, offered individual sessions but the awkward reality came piercing through in handful of words mumbled by the Sachem in passing one tired afternoon.

"I guess you can't teach talent," he said, trucking toward his dome.

It was no secret Pierre had come from another place. A different hunting ground. In the full season since his arrival he'd been asked more times about catching than his first name. Deeply concerned with what he was rather than who, and how could he blame them. Pierre Oiseau didn't mean nearly as much as 'King Catcher.' They said it with reverence. He was their gift. Retribution from the stars for taking so many some time ago. The Lack, their ebb and Pierre, their flow.

Unfortunately, the Sachem had it wrong on one account. It wasn't talent. It was evolution. Pierre wasn't better by just skill or repetition. Like the prey evolved to avoid being caught, the Falklands race evolved to catch them. Here there was no risk. No scarcity of food. No direct consequence for failure. Here, they wouldn't starve for lack of bounty but rather the insufficient ability to catch it. If they didn't get all they needed on the first go round, they'd simply go out and try again. Again and again until exhaustion. But when you have only one chance to get it right, one opportunity, it had to be perfect. You hunt with the fuel of desperation. That was what Pierre couldn't turn off. The motor hardwired to his aggression.

The Catchers worked profusely, showing glints of progress though sluggish and unsubstantial. They were no doubt becoming better. Stronger swimmers, an improved tactical team, extended wind capacity, but their free flow instincts, accuracy of senses, and reactions in the moment still paled in comparison to where they needed to be. There is no prize for effort. No one can live on that. They had to meet the call. As time wore on he saw his failure day in, day out, having to approach it with a false encouraging smile.

Watching the crew go sun up to sun down fed a slow digging depression. The population was on the run, growing rapidly within the last weeks. The line at the Reserve stretched along the beach, the evening swim spread further East and wider West. Pierre swore he saw ten fresh bodies a day. Youth talking as if his title was their first words, jawing the three syllables, raising a pointed flipper wide-eyed and off-balance, inexperienced with their new bodies. Standing in front of the Reserve, Pierre turned to the diminished collection of food for the day. He plucked out the last one, and scooped it over to a fluffy grey fledgling. As he stood watching her trip thrice in five steps, Pierre leaned against the depleted Reserve. His gaze hung, beginning to realize the truth.

He was trapped.

Chapter 32

Stopping short of the faded silver dome Patricia centered herself for the worst. Despite her soft emotions, she had to be his rock. For Tiberius, flight was his life, his strap of pride, and to be grounded hurt her almost as much as him. Stepping inside, the sand looked like small frozen waves colored in tan. Ghostly mute acoustics cocooned the hollow from the outside world. Everything within was heard with disturbing definition, as her footsteps patted and crunched the delicate grains. Tiberius across the circular room laid on a bed of large ovular dark green leaves. His neck slowly turned and his small black eyes listlessly watched Patricia approach.

"Nice twirl, but you could've stuck the landing," she said, stopping a few steps short.

Tiberius grunted and made a cumbersome roll onto his side. The loose round rocks of his bed clicked and slid against one another.

"The medics said you told them you hit a storm, and were thrown down on Bouvet. Others say you said you were mauled on the Falklands. You remember what happened?"

"It's a bit blurry."

"How do you feel now?"

His gaze fell to the floor.

"We don't have to discuss it. I'm just glad you're in good condition."

He nodded. There was a silence.

"Okay, well, they said I should let you rest. So." She leaned over and patted him on the head. "I'll visit tomorrow." She turned for the opening.

"Patricia," he asked concerned. "I can leave, right?"

His words hung in the empty space. Patricia pivoted. "What do you mean?"

"I mean, if I wanted to."

"You could, but those wings will take time. Besides how would you eat? Where would you sleep? It's not safe outside here."

"The Falklands aren't safe, you let me fly there."

"Because I trust my brother would let nothing happen to you."

He swallowed, rolling onto his back. "What happens if I can't run errands anymore? What do I become?" He was looking up at the ceiling.

"We'll have to wait and see."

"What do you think will happen?"

"I don't know," she said with a drop in her voice. "I don't know."

OISEAU THE KING CATCHER

Chapter 33

Whenever he closed his eyes he saw himself falling from a gold-plated sky. Flailing, yelling, crashing into rough sand. A small gawking party on the shore like orbiting black spots watched him plummet. The vision stopped with the small explosion of specks. Then picked back up as a troop of medics pushed their way through a condensed crowd, pausing, looking down on his bent wings and twisted back. The ground jumped, as a tall furry giant joined the crowd. It reached down and blocked the sun.

The next morning he awoke mummified in kelp being told he could only leave for short breaks. His quarters in the Wellness Ward were an arched bastille. He hated every pale grey wall, each side resembling the other. He missed the caw of gulls, the chatter of penguins, the rolling smash of open sea. This place was an eerie asylum.

There wasn't any work for him since Patricia placed his runs on hold. She visited every morning, carrying in her mouth a special fish for him to try or novelties she found patrolling the island. She was his only tie to the outside world, and the gaps between her visits drove him stir-crazy. He was used to being busy, having missions and distractions, but in the silence, there was time to think. About Solus. About their conversation. About his future.

He had 49 nights of recovery before he *should* be able to fly. Should was the word he could've done without. If they were wrong, he had nothing to contribute. Nothing to offer. Of what use is a grounded bird? How long before the pity waned and they started to call for his Banishment? What could Patricia really do to hold them off without herself becoming a hypocrite? His chest was pumping.

It saddened him to think of the citizens as 'them', but he remembered how it was before. Before they found out what he had to give, before he had purpose. He remembered what they were prepared to do. He didn't want to betray Patricia, but he didn't want to go back to what he was, and he was running out of time. Being on the wrong side of this when it came to pass was life and death. Tiberius lay there, staring up at the dome and sighed. Solus made a proposal, and he had a choice.

Chapter 34

The albatross' condition robbed Pierre dearly. The weekly report provided was the only news he had of home. The once impeccable bird, with blinding white feathers perfectly aligned, was now mangled, dirty and discolored. Wraps of seaweed covered his chest mixed with tinged green and dried blood spilling blots of oxford. Pierre barely recognized Patricia's confidant as he pulled up next to him at the Reserve.

"This isn't fair," Tiberius said, the booming voice now shriveled and faint.

"I'm sorry for what happened," Pierre replied.

"Not this," Tiberius snipped, waving a bent appendage across his stale wounds. "This is collateral. This is my duty. What's unfair is how any of us would have to be in a place against our will."

"Some of us don't have the power to change our situations."

"I believed that once. But I've come to learn power comes in steps. From doing what you have to, even when it's uncomfortable."

Pierre frowned. "What do you mean?"

"I've seen your parents, talked to them. They miss you very much." Tiberius touched Pierre's shoulder. "The same expressions they have, I see on you. This was never meant to be permanent. This was a temporary arrangement, one day ending in you leaving forever. But maybe to do that you'll have to play a part."

"How?"

"Has anyone ever told you about the Great Excavation?"

Pierre shook his head.

Tiberius sneered, rolling his eyes. "Typical. It's an event, at the end of the mating season."

"What happens?"

"I've never been. I'm told it's a celebration. Seabirds from every culture come to share in knowledge, flavor, and games. A place, usually meant for fun, but in your case…"

"You think someone might know about the war?"

Tiberius shrugged. "Who knows? They come from all over. What would be your loss?"

Pierre felt himself grasping at frail hope, but with the Messenger grounded, no other option gave him none at all.

The albatross raised a brow. "If you never go how can you know? I'm no use to you in this condition, and likely won't ever be use to you again."

Pierre was unaware the damage was that extensive.

"No one else is willing to fly to your homeland, and can you fault them?" The bird looked himself over. "What do you have to lose? Seize your own opportunities, or trust me, you could be here forever."

They surveyed the glistening paradise with dry expressions. A beautiful home.

"Where is it?" Pierre finally asked.

Tiberius smiled. "South side of Bouvet. Two rises of the sun." Then the bird turned and painfully labored off.

Despite not having an in-depth conversation before now, with any news always filtered in code through Patricia, Pierre developed a fond respect for Tiberius' risks for his family. A mesh of stories circulated the Cape about how the bird came upon his strange assortment of injuries. The most popular being he was attacked on the Falklands delivering the message. What faintly stumped Pierre was how he got back so fast and in such a condition, returning the same day he left? He was a swift albatross, but is that possible?

That conundrum mattered less than no one telling him of the Great Excavation. Why didn't they say something? With citizens enveloped in their families and elites worried about national safety, perhaps it was possible it slipped their minds. Possible. Regardless, he was glad Tiberius thought to make him aware. A mounting excitement churned as his sparkling imagination dabbled. Pierre bounced on his toes in a joyful gambol. How strange life can change. Cogitation, merry and wishful led to the same glorious end. *What if?*

Chapter 35

Impatience can ruin an otherwise worthy plan. In the time following his talk with the albatross, Solus prepared. Everything had to be flawless. The harsh unwavering climate on the island shaved him to a skeleton. Less daunting, more haunting, yet still inflamed with the vigor of the condemned. The three pectoral marks completely scarred over along with the engravings in his shoulder from Banishment. Solus admired the slightly raised tissue on his chest, stroking it gently. This was well earned. Rattled by a dawning epiphany and fear for his life, the albatross spilled very pertinent details. Information quivered off his beak and Solus picked up a nugget equal to a treasury.

For it, the albatross wanted a trade. Only one plea, his freedom during the coup. Once the Cape surrendered, Tiberius was promised to be saved during the uprising, and have a place of high regard within the new system. A small sacrifice. Solus agreed, under the condition Tiberius could perform a singular task successfully. The Fiordland entered the Great Excavation, steeping with contempt. He scanned the perimeter, and approached the section beaming with color.

OISEAU THE KING CATCHER

Chapter 36

As the penguins of Caterwaul docked on Bouvet, wiggling themselves dry, Pierre paused at the edge. The jagged glacial mountains he remembered, worked to bisect the island, separating Paul's seclusion from the robust attractions of the penguin world fair. Citizens scattered like miscreants to their pleasures, crossing Pierre's path as he lingered trying to make sense of some icy engravings on the ground. A glistening roadmap, trampled by the more experienced but heeded reverently by first timers. They huddled, necks curved. Arrows spread like a peacock display in six directions with sections of the event: Toboggan Trails (Left), Battle Arena (Diagonal Left), Sea Treats (Straight Left), Wonder Cure (Straight Right), Scavenger Sect (Diagonal Right), Garment District (Right).

A good chunk of the colony was in attendance but the only ones Pierre actually knew were the two he hunted with. His aunt and uncle stayed home, confessing their vacation was when the Cape went on one. 'The beauty without the busy,' they claimed, even when asked separately.

Aria opted to remain behind, helping Sachem and Puddles so Pierre could have her slot. The official story was she didn't care for the event like she used to. Pierre thought that only half true, and was grateful for her generosity. She was heartedly ambiguous but poorly hid her charity.

As Xander impatiently explained en route, the Great Excavation was once a year. The festivities were a privilege not a right and newcomers were required to forfeit their first term to show patriotism. Pierre sensed Xander's aggravation. Pierre was sure in Xander's eyes him being allowed to come his first year was but another exception applied to the King from the Falklands. He envied what he did not understand. With half the Cape going at a time, taking turns, it meant only fifty percent of the provisions were necessary. This was the season for eager understudies in every department to practice some real fieldwork. Moreover, keeping a populated presence on the Cape was imperative to deterring squatters. With access to forest and ocean, Tree Dwellers, albatross, a controlled point of entry, and scarce natural predators, Caterwaul's geography had drawn a saturated lust. Location, perhaps as much as any other factor, probably aided in the building of their great society.

But every society, no matter how great, required an outlet. An unchecked release to peel them away from their typical areas and typical selves. The Excavation was the molting of the mundane.

Could something like this have helped the Falklands to appreciate one another rather than fight? Even the thought was a waste.

The Falklands was a cultural quarantine. A grim grey nimbus obstructing your view of everything beyond. Pierre only recognized the aviary from the outside, and never so clearly as right now. Yet in that cage there was comfort, the familiar. Caterwaul was the true prison.

Tiberius noted that the event lasted two arcs of the sun. Pierre doubted that was enough time to take in all it had to offer. Struggling not to get lost in the majesty, the tourist planted himself in a busy intersection and got to work digging for intelligence. In the width of several seconds he was bumped, brushed, and shoved. Regaining his composure each time, he shredded vexation. Brief gaps between the crowds showed the fullness of the event with a blast of cold air, and a bright, crisp visual.

Penguins, shops, towering mountains, nods and smiles, laughter and running. The blinding white met artic blue to form a backdrop traversed by birds of every colony and clan. Then, it closed up again, the space filling with bodies mixing to and fro. Pierre returned to his duty, pulling his gaze from the distance on honing on his immediate surroundings. Tirelessly he canvassed, surveying those around him. Most never looked up. Others, rushed by devoid of sound, and the ones who did have words, didn't have very pleasant ones.

Penguins didn't come to be bothered, Pierre surmised. Not wanting to dwell on wars or sad foreign places with dark foreign troubles. Elation was the desired matrix, loose, easy, free. Whatever threatened that notion was pummeled and scolded, much like Pierre's interrogation.

The day wore on and emptiness grew with every shake of the head. His flesh hung heavier on his bones with each shrug of the shoulder and aggravated wave. Consumed by their own agendas, they were rushing past before he could even finish his sentence. Those who crossed his path before walked wide around, staring at Pierre, circling him like a roundabout. His throat was dry and weary. Endurance beaten from his muscles, natural fatigue robbed him his vivacity, and the once spirited inquisition shortened in length, from 'Do you know of the war in the Falklands?' to, 'The war in the Falklands?' to, 'The Falklands?' The more Pierre asked the more he realized the ubiquitous ignorance about his home and its wearies. He was lost. This event prided itself on being a meeting of every known colony on Earth and yet was oblivious to the rampant chaos just across the ocean. Perpetual blank stares proved to Pierre the world was only what you know of it.

The depleted islander drug to the nearest section and collapsed. After gazing at a soft tuft of snow between his feet, he looked up, asking the Macaroni his question.

The cheerful round-faced attendant shook his head, but leaned over the block of rectangular ice and started talking. "We've got an incredible delicacy this go-round." He arched his eyebrows. "A pack of wild penguins off the coast of Tasmania brought us a real treat. Shark!"

Pierre narrowed his eyes.

"Would ya like to know how they did it?"

Before Pierre could respond the vendor was underway. "One lured the shark in to a location, okay okay, where, waiting in ambush were six companions. Right? Their beaks sharpened to pikes, and they hovered." The bird did a weird oscillating body wave. "When gills were fully exposed, they lanced! And lanced! And lanced and lanced and lanced and lanced and labalalala." He shook his face. Wide-eyed starting to drool. Then leaned back and calmed down. "Until the leviathan spilt over. Environmentalists call them savages. Self-righteous punks. I," he beat his chest, dragging the vowel, "call them artists." The Macaroni focused. "So, you want to try it?"

Pierre stood, scanning the assortment. A scrumptious organized assortment. The sights cooed to his grumbling stomach, but as he swayed his beak over the prime cuts, something gave him pause.

Amongst other animals, sharks ate penguins. And here he was, possibly out of some form of retribution, to eat what would've eaten him. He looked at the meat. He might know someone in there. Without quite being able to put it into words, devouring parts of the chopped Mako sounded like second-rate cannibalism.

"I'll have something else," Pierre said, shaking the thought.

The connoisseur straightened from his lean and lowered his eyes. "Oh. What would your expert tastes prefer?" There was salt in his tone.

The massive variety made choosing difficult. Absolutely nothing looked normal about the array. Beige Stargazer, Orange Wrasse, Blue Runner, Green Dragonet, silver Sargo, red Striped Weever, and more Pierre was just introduced to. Being selective suddenly felt important. Pierre rocked his weight. He didn't want to expose his brute pallet, but so much of what he saw was estranged to him. Challenging the attendant's offer forced him to make a sophisticated decision of his own. He clinched his cheeks, tapping his beak. Wanting to prove he was better than the server thought. That he wasn't a savage, that he knew stuff. Prove he was sophisticated, classy, diverse. He wasn't. In fact he was extra regular. His true favorite was common and base.

Pierre stood over a neatly laid collection hmm'ing and ahh'ing. The Macaroni cocked his head to the side and sighed, apparently tired of the bourgeois theatrics. Without looking Pierre pointed down and across his body to the left, analyzing the attendant. The penguin leaned back and winced. Pierre examined his selection. Black and white Inkfin. The attendant held a long lingering look.

Pierre's gaze darted left and right, then he held his chin high, confirming with a stiff nod. The vendor, contorted his face into annoyed expressions, then stepped back and laughed. Pierre laughed too, though not sure at what. He slid the King penguin a half dozen of the portion.

"You've made a good choice."

Pierre loosed his shoulders, took his food, and sunk to the ground. He nibbled on the fish with the sweet tang. Not so sure what the attendant said was true. The day was a waste. Pierre had learned nothing of value as the sun was well into its descent. He was content to settle there, a gluttonous, defeated stranger humbled for the rest of the evening until something caught his eye. Through spots in the bustling crowd, a vision pulled him to his feet.

Chapter 37

Sudden and unannounced. Imposing and rude. If he readied all his life for this moment, he'd still be unprepared. No matter where in the world this happened the reaction would be the same. He felt guilt. There was so much to do. He moved to walk away. His functions stuck. He went to ask a stranger his usual questions, a polite Rockhopper who actually stopped and addressed him. But all Pierre could manifest was garbled onomatopoeia. What was wrong? Mr. Oiseau was completely distracted. What was this, this thing, this, this elixir? Why was it happening now? There couldn't be a worse time.

She turned and caught a glimpse across the walkway. He ducked. Standing behind nothing. *She saw me*! He wanted to run. Each pathetic, lousy webbed foot was of no use. She was coming! Why! He looked at his orange feet, cursing them with slander. His father's courting words echoed in his head. Not because it was good, but because it was the only direction he had: 'Start with your left, you'll do your best. Start with your right, you'll be all right.' What the hell did that mean? Pierre debated the better of the two while he moved in a salsa. One in front of the other, slow and unsure, before jerking it back and replacing it with the other. He bore a serious frown. Soft wind and light breath announced a body very close.

"Are you all right?"

Pierre raised his head to shimmering emerald eyes. His verbs and nouns hitched and popped like old equipment.

"Are you all right?" she repeated, her tone more concerned.

"Aaaa." He nodded, staring.

She looked as though she bit into something bitter. "I thought you had a condition. What's wrong with your feet?"

"Hmm?"

"Your feet!"

Pierre looked down. They still moved. He snapped them still. Stupid feet.

"I was coming to show you to the medics," she said.

"The medics?"

She looked him up, down, back up, then motioned for him to follow. He hustled to keep pace. They work now, he mocked. She approached a booth with seven small Fairy penguins so similar in appearance they could be each other.

"They call this the Wonder Cure department. Yet every time I come here I wonder why there's not a cure," she bellowed to the attendants.

"So-rry, Em-ily," the workers respond in unison like a small class.

"We're working on it," one replied before vanishing behind two others.

Pierre assumed he was the leader, for no other reason than for a moment, he was up front.

"I know," she said, "I'm just roughing you up. A quip of humor is the only thing that keeps me sane, and," she raised a wing, "from on a back-slapping frenzy. Running through the crowd and popping the face off of everything." Emily started a slow-motion demonstration. Moving in exaggerated steps, stopping every few cycles to give a taste of her flipper with real-time commentary.

Smmmack! "What you say?" *Pap-Pap!* "Oh, you want some too?" *Hyuh!*

Pierre laughed. Her eyes glinted, telling her fabled wishes. This Gentoo was crazy, but also the prettiest thing he'd ever seen.

Pierre managed to talk through a chuckle. "Why do you want to pop penguins you don't even know?"

"Because they've had it better than me, and I can hear them complain about it."

"Mm," Pierre grunted, "I know what you mean."

"Do you?"

He found the calm to look at her without staring.

She frowned. "Why are you here?"

"I'm searching for something."

"So is everyone. Why are you here?"

"I have some questions, but no one seems to know the answers."

"Mm," she grunted, "I know what you mean." She was staring.

"Do you?"

She raised her flipper. He cowered. "Why are you here?"

"Answers."

"Maybe we can trade questions."

"Or we could make our own solutions"

Pierre felt warm. Hot blood rushed his face.

"I know what you need," she said, standing closer now.

Pierre swallowed. He looked down, leaning forward.

"Follow me." She left.

Chapter 38

Navigating the populous, they snaked down a path and came to the foot of a steep trail. The sparkling snow had prints primarily in one direction, with a few staggering impressions coming toward them.

"Cowards," she muttered.

Pierre examined them wondering why so many went up, and so few came down. Grey rocks lined the outside of the road bending where the eye could not follow. As he walked toward the sky, the noise he had hardly noticed before fell further and further away. Pierre didn't know where he was going or cared. The day rewarded him not for his efforts, and today he had no more efforts to give. Tomorrow, he promised. Tomorrow would be the day. Their conversation was constant. Honest and unforced. Like talking to someone who could tell no one of importance. Slowly, she got around to lapses in her mother's memory. Slowly, he got around to talking about home. They made their ascent, carried by a surprising exchange.

"Wanna know a secret?" she asked, cutting through Pierre's rant on Mackerel and its glory.

"Sometimes, you don't get an answer or a cure, sometimes you just have to cope."

Pierre opened to address the theory, but in the approaching the summit, the skyline broke. The water looked like a massive pool, clouds crossed the sky in herds as a ball of light shone through splitting itself into smaller parts. A tingling draft brushed over his body. Emily planted one foot in front of the other in an accomplished stance, panting slightly. She stared off into the endless visage as if looking for the face of her maker.

Pierre pulled alongside slightly more winded than he wanted to let on. Water fitness, he learned, was not like land fitness. Running on the remains of a day full of solicitation, the only thing that carried him was the chatter. He stood, poorly erect, speaking through unattractive beak-breathing.

"Or maybe," he finally said, "the merchants, don't have, what you need. Maybe, the answer isn't to stop life, but to find a way, to move with it." He struggled to lift a flipper. "Even when it's hard."

"Easy for you to say," she shot, stepping on his words. "Both your parents are still alive."

"You promise?" He was still unable to catch his breath and still trying to mask it, speaking loud through unattractive beak breathing. This climb was much taller than his perch in Caterwaul.

He plopped down and she followed, her gentle gaze upon him.

"If it's bad, why don't they leave? Are they afraid?"

"Of what they'd leave behind. They believe home is something worth saving."

"A place is only as good as its penguins."

"I believe that too. That's why I want to go back. I'm in this paradise now, you can see it there." He pointed to the two titanic beige mountains, visible across the stretch of water. "No war, no lack food, I can live a hero the rest of my life, but I don't want it. Not because I lust for battle or have nostalgia about hunger pains, I miss them. I just miss them. I'd trade these blue skies in an instant."

"Why don't you?"

"They risked a lot to get me away."

"Ah. I don't think you're living in misery so you can be polite. Please. What's the real reason?"

Pierre took a pause. "They depend on me now."

"Who?"

"The colony."

Emily sat back and for a long while said nothing. "Is it better not knowing?"

"I would rather be able to cherish what time I have, than to have none at all."

"At least it comes with hope. The other side of your guess. You can believe what you want. Good or bad. You don't want to see your parents how I have to see my mother. To be in that pain with them."

"I'm not much better without them."

Pierre never had a real talk about home since he was sent away. Short debriefings with those more curious than caring about the facts, but never about the feeling. Possibly, she was the only one who cared.

"Welp," Emily said, hopping to her feet as she stretched her back, "while you're here, in this blissful miserable place, make the most of it." Her pace changed. She swung her flippers, seeming to be in a rush. "Ever been Tobogganing?" Emily glanced down at him.

The wind on the mountaintop now dry and chilling. Pierre stood, peering over the cliff, bending his neck to follow steep curves. Visitors below looked like wandering black specks on a light blue backdrop. "I've seen it done," he said with assurance. He hadn't. But it sounded better than the truth of him being scared pale at the thought. The maniacal first drop made him want to crawl into an egg.

"Good, let's go," she said with a pop.

His eyes bulged. "Oh. No. No, no, no, I—I just wanted to walk you up."

"I walked you up."

"And now I have. Long day. Just ate." He patted his stomach. "Umm. See you at the bottom?"

Emily rolled her eyes. "Sand penguins are such sissyfoots when it comes to the Trails. I don't know wh—Ah!" Emily shrieked, breaking her even tone, lost, gazing over the cliff.

In his cowardly stammer Pierre had unconsciously inched several feet back. "What is it?" he said in a heavy voice, not budging from his distance.

Emily remained mute, focusing below. She swallowed hard, twisted her face, shaking her head. Pierre moved, sliding his webbed feet along the smooth ice instead of picking them up.

She screamed, pointing down into a swarm of dots. He rushed to her side.

"What?"

"There!"

"Where!"

"There!" She was hopping.

"Where?" he asked, nervously scanning.

"Right...there."

Pierre noticed two things: A sharp drop in her voice and a hard thump in his back. For a full three seconds his body touched nothing. Freefalling parallel to the mountainside. A smooth arc of the ice came up to meet the descent as his belly touched with the slope. When he found the courage to open both eyes, Emily was on his left. Rushing on the wide reflective half-pipe, streamlined, with both her wings cocked to the side. A small curve approached through sparse flurries. Pierre crashed into the bend, tumbling helplessly before slamming back on his stomach. Emily tilted her figure in rhythm and zipped around the curve. Skimming her claws atop the ice, she aligned with Pierre.

"Drop left foot to go left. Drop right, to—" a whipping wind stole her words and carried them up the mountain.

Pierre's cheeks felt like they were blown to the back of his face. He swerved and cut, trying to get a hold of the controls. Emily lifted her anchors and jetted out in front. Another bend blitzed them through the trail. Emily took it high, sliding to the top before slanting down with bonus momentum. Pierre wanted to follow suit, but couldn't stop wiggling until the wall was in front of his beak.

He jammed a foot down in panic, hooking a rigid left into the curve. He slid limply up the surface before flopping over on his back. As he lay there upside down, heading south, tired and out of breath, ready to forfeit and go home, he noticed he was gaining velocity. Was there no end? The prolonged fright caused a numbing effect. Pierre accepted whatever was going to come and braced for the pain and embarrassment. Rocking left to right he tried to roll over. Lifting his neck to see what torment lay ahead, he saw nothing. An upside-down sky, an island below, and the distant sea. No left curve, no right curve, no ice. No Ice? Pierre fumbled right-side up, guessing it must be a trick of the horizon. An eternity away, a small beautiful speck catapulted into oblivion.

Pierre dropped off another cliff. He flapped his wings frenetically, hoping they'd catch wind. But the thick condensed stretches of bones covered in skin-tight feather were more like oars than sails. Built for water, not air. He spun in diagonal front flips before the slope came to catch him. A short white ramp was ahead thinly shrouded by a misty grey breeze, after which…nothing. Just a deep dip down, a short tilt up, and farewell, to a cruel cruel world. Pierre had survived a civil war, a leopard seal, and Sherri only to be defeated by a crazy pretty bird who pushed him off a mountain.

The fall was merciless and fast. His innards sank. The sky and ocean bled together in one incomprehensible blur as water trickled from the sides of his eyes. In a glitch, everything shifted up. He couldn't no longer feel the ice running along his belly. He looked. It wasn't there.

Chapter 39

Ground. Slope. Ocean. All dropped away as he launched through cold air. Instinctively, he flapped again. It was all he knew to do. This time though, it worked. He was actually flying! A dream of swimming through the sky had come true. The weightlessness was euphoric. Not like the thick sluggish liquid, which did everything it could to hold him back. This was free. Uninhibited. He wished he could always feel like this.

As the sensations of life sparked at their peak, his ascent slowed. The wind in his ear churned to a stop as it took an intermission. Pierre observed a stillness of the world like never before. He closed his eyes, begging for it to stay. But as his beak tilted back toward the earth, gravity snatched him for a hug. The loud ruffle of air in his ear rose until it was deafening. Everything below was a bright white. He couldn't make sense of where he was going, or how fast he was getting there, or why someone would do something like this?

Toboggan Trails, where penguins come to live before they die. Falling was a lot faster than rising, as it often tends to be, and before he knew it Pierre was wondering where everybody went.

Where were the vendors? Where were the visitors? Where was Emily? He plunged into a thicket of colorlessness, as something humongous swallowed him whole. His rapid velocity was pacified into a pleasant tumble, rolling him out the other side of snow. The festive commotion reconvened, along with a radiant Gentoo tapping her left foot.

"You okay?" Emily's voice echoed, somewhere close.

Disoriented from the dips, whips, and drops, Pierre panned for the source. The dizziness ebbed, as three Emilies disappointingly phased into two, then one. He could only hyperventilate, and look at her like a cat doused in water. Her, a lunatic, getting her cheap thrills from unsuspecting sand penguins. Lying at the base of her rollercoaster, he blinked for long periods of time. Tuning in to the rapping of her foot, Pierre noticed something odd. She wasn't sympathetic. She wasn't apologetic. She was impatient. What was she waiting for? Pierre swallowed hard and then finally shook his head slightly in response to the question posed moments ago. He was okay, but he wasn't going to let her know that. He had a rational hesitance of what she might do or want to do next.

"Shut up, you liked it," she said, apparently seeing through the facade. Emily now expressed that she had been riding the trails for years when her mother would take her before the illness. She admitted having the same exact look the first time she rolled out of the snow pile. Privately thinking her mom was jealous of her youthful good looks and had plotted to 'off' her on the slopes. But once she came through the other side frightened, discombobulated, ruffled but ultimately safe she realized she had the best time of her life. Only the fear of the unknown that can put that kind of look on a penguin's face. Then she admitted Pierre was right. It is better to know. So you can enjoy the ride.

"Took long enough getting down here," she said with a sass.

"I'm glad there was a down here," Pierre mumbled, his breaths more spaced out. "I thought I was going to die."

"You are," she offered with a devilish macabre smile. "Just not today. Now come on, let's do it again."

Pierre jabbered senselessly, the rebuttal pure mush. Before he knew it he was being forcefully prodded, waddling back toward the walkway. Like a youth who had just taken a playful beating going back in for seconds. Pierre was once that penguin, jumping on his brother's back as soon as he got home from the front lines. To have Craig's well-trained reflexes and strong physique toss him cross the cave. Only then for Pierre to roll over giggling and stumbling, coming off-balance for more. The truth was, he did like the Toboggan. It was the most fun he ever had and now, waddling toward the summit was the first time he'd laughed this laugh. Light, unrestricted. Nothing behind, nothing beneath. Free.

In that moment, he grasped the tough decision his parents made to send him away. This was what they were talking about that night in the cave. This was why they took the risk. For him to be happy, fully. Since leaving the Falklands, this moment was the first time he was exactly where he wanted to be.

They climbed and rode the Trails ten times that fateful day, with the newness of what they'd discovered giving fresh vie. On the last trip up, they paused to watch the sun give a triumphant bow before retiring for the evening. As they sat, breathing in the falling twilight atop the highest mountain, Pierre never wanted to come down. A star-covered dome arched around them, and they wrapped themselves up in it. Solidifying their bond with a different kind of dance, declaring softly to one another what they already knew. Pierre didn't find what he was looking for that day on Bouvet but when he wasn't looking something found him. Love.

Chapter 40

Morning came like a warm alarm. It was the last day of the Great Excavation and in his heart Pierre was still committed to searching, but the desperate vigor he once possessed had gravely wilted. That drive now having to share space. His mind wanted dearly to hold on to his past, but everything he felt was lost in last night and prying his thoughts from Emily was like trying to take a fish from Puddles.

Waking up was a slow disappointing bloom. The dull orange morning came with reality. Their obligations and circumstance, this tattered series of events that shaped their lives. Truth was, she had to go her way, and he had to go his. Emily had already stayed out past her curfew from a mother who lacked self-sufficiency. Her mission for medicine, again, was unsuccessful, and the descent this go round took more than physical will. He could see it in her eyes, and he'd known it would show in his. They wanted to hide up there. From who they were and who they were supposed to be. Decency and nobility weren't a fair trade, and doing the right thing was a frail reward compared to what they just experienced. But sharing that same gaze, the wide-eyed fear gave way to a sagging guilt, and they knew they were going to be better than they wanted.

They weren't going to take the slide down, wanting this to last. As they walked the wet snow, within its guidelines of rocks, the conversation didn't resemble the day before. The communication was constant yet without words. They made a covenant on that mountain, a promise, a pact both thought could not break. He'd found no one like her across the sea. Reaching the bottom, Pierre noticed they were now those first steps going against the grain. Just yesterday Emily had called the owners of such footsteps cowards. Perhaps she was right. Bending to the left they passed by a long booth he never noticed the day before. Pierre took a deft detour and Emily followed.

"What-can-I-do-for ya?" a slim Magellanic blurted so fast it sounded like one word.

It took Pierre seconds to compute. The keeper had feathers that swirled black and white as he stood, looking everywhere but forward.

"I want to get something for my..." Pierre hesitated, then continued, "mate." He wasn't bold enough to check her reaction but in his mind, she might've blushed.

"There is no getting, only winning."

"Winning?"

"Winning."

"How?"

"Riddles."

"Riddles?"

"Where's the echo? Riddles."

"Okay."

"Unlike the brutes over at the Battle Arena, bashing their brains out for scant machismo, *we* champion intellect."

Pierre opened his beak.

"Yes, intellect," the keeper repeated.

Pierre exhaled.

"Answer all three you get a prize."

"What if I answer two?"

"A compliment."

"One?"

"Sarcasm."

"None?"

"Unflappable disrespect. You ready?"

"If I lose can I try again?"

"Maybe if she asks."

Emily leaned in. "If we lose can we try again?"

"No. First riddle: There is a word of letters three, add two and fewer there will be."

Emily whispered into his ear, "It's a trick. You can't add to something and have less of it."

Pierre stared. It was tough to concentrate with her so near.

"Maybe," he finally said, "the word won't be less, but whatever it's referring to. These things thrive off simplicity. We have to think in reverse." Pierre tapped his beak and lifted his head.

"Few."

The attendant looked off. "Huh?"

"Few!"

He narrowed his eyes.

Emily bounced. "Well!"

"Second riddle."

They let out all the breath in their lungs.

The attendant cleared his throat and raised his voice. "Ahem. Second. Riddle."

They nodded.

"You heard me before yet you hear me again. Then I die, till you call again."

Being raised in caves Pierre couldn't help but laugh when he hypothesized an answer. Whenever permitted, they'd howl for evenings, saying absolutely nothing of purpose, fascinated by the acoustic response. What lived in those deep dark places saying whatever you'd say so well you couldn't tell your voice from its? Emily right on his shoulder was excited by the devious smile.

"An echo."

193

Emily hopped brimming with glee. "I've never won! I've never won!" she spouted.

The attendant eyeballed her, lifting his chin. "And you still haven't."

"Is it correct?" Pierre said, commanding the bird's focus.

"The true test of a mind is not depth but diversity." The attendant tapped the tips of his wings together, put his chin in his chest, then looked up. "It's more colorful than anything seen, and not a penguin can touch it, not even a King."

Pierre stared at the ice. Emily at Pierre. Their gazes met and his fell back to the floor.

The attendant smiled and stepped up. "Hmm?"

"Um."

"Hmm!" he said more forcefully.

Pierre searched his partner.

"I thought so," the keeper said turning around.

Pierre had to say something. They were running out of time. "Sunse—"

"Rainbow!" Emily shrieked.

The bird pivoted angrily. He scowled, his face crumpled into a clump. "Come again," he said.

"It's a rainbow."

He snorted like a bull shaking his head. Then after a moment, stepped aside. Parting a troop of ornery seabirds standing guard twelve paces back, he escorted Pierre and Emily into the vault.

"Welcome to the Scavenger's Spiral," he said, grumbling.

A layout of prizes swirled in the snow, out from its center like a giant seashell. Orange-Red Feathers, sparkling blue gems, a giant bronze egg tall as Pierre, dazzling white cloaks, rare purple flowers, pointed silver sticks, and more. Emily and Pierre walked the wide curved path sprinkled with collector's items as the keeper turned curator, explaining each piece they showed interest in. Its known history, usages, and method of procurement. The quick-tongued Megellanic was a profound database for all oddities of the sea. Emily perused giddily, touching, moving, and tipping sometimes adding the occasional yip. She sputtered half-finished sentences, ignoring them both as she wandered the white treasured garden. An array of trinkets, each as undiscovered to them as the next.

Pierre browsed the cache, equally impressed as he was ignorant until one stopped him in his tracks. "What is it?" he asked. Emily rushed over and caught up to the group.

"This little doo-dad drifted south of the Canary current, got picked up by the Brazilian current and wound up on the South Georgias. A traveler with our crew, who had done some hard time in an Australian aquarium, said he'd seen visitors carry something like that around their neck. That's how I think you're supposed to wear it. Around your neck. We've tinkered with it for some time and…" He signaled to two workers who picked up the prize without breaking stride and floated toward Pierre. "Slip the loop over your head like so, down to your shoulders." Pierre stooped as they put on the soft, smooth contraption. "Then pull gently with your beak to tighten, and clamp the loose part here."

"Why anyone would wear such a thing is strange to me, but that's how he said he'd seen it and dagnabbit that's how it's done!" The crew slid back. Once adjusted it was like a golden butterfly, wings spread sitting atop his chest.

"It's beautiful," Emily said.

"But I came to win you a prize."

"I don't need two prizes." Emily turned to the curator. "We'll take this one."

Before the group dispersed, Pierre had them remove the reward and give it to his partner. He had to stay with the Cape, and she had to stay with her mother. While held in separate worlds, this would be a token of their promise. They resolved to meet every Excavation. Pierre didn't care about the colony's rotation rule. He was coming. He walked her to the departure point for Antarctica and they rubbed their necks together in silence. As she took her leave Pierre smiled and sank. There was nothing left here. He made his peace.

Wandering back through the maze, he worked his way to the other side of the island. From a rest area near the Garment District, a sound buzzed while Pierre moved through the scattered assembly that gave him no choice but to pause. He continued, and it buzzed again, this time stopping him in his steps. It hung. Unmistakable. Impossible for him to ignore. Syllables he thought he'd never hear.

Chapter 41

Pierre twisted, tracking the words. He checked his imagination, then he checked again as he stumbled drunkenly on the conversation of strangers. One was talking very loud to a close audience, while the other seemed half attentive to the exchange. Pierre, however, was drawn like a ship to a Siren.

A penguin stood, shades of grey, purple, and black orbiting his body. One of the suitors draping themselves in wraps from the Garment District to stand out and appear more attractive. With such a dazzling hue, he was clearly here searching to find someone for the season. His vocal patterns pumped excitement, as words tipped and rolled. The top half of his back crouched over, his neck slung long and low having to look up at penguins that otherwise would've been shorter than he was if he were standing straight.

"Did you say Falklands?" Pierre asked, interrupting what was more of a monologue.

The colorful bird turned around in more steps than it should take anyone to do so and pointed his focus at the King. "I did. Do you know of the place?"

"I'm from there," Pierre said, poking out his chest before rescinding a little.

"Yea? Are you the fellow that's been asking all the questions?" the stranger queried with a smile.

"I am," Pierre said, excited his interrogations yielded fruit but a little embarrassed at the same time.

"Come closer so I can look at you." The bent bird circled Pierre like a specimen. "Right height," mumble mumble mumble, "right weight," mumble mumble. He peeked under his chin. "Right kind." He shuffled back for a full view. "By golly, you are. Delio Egnever, ecstatic to find you, you're just as he described!"

"Who?"

"Well, Paul Jaunty of course."

"You know Paul!" Pierre yelled, flinging his beak over both shoulders. "Is he here?"

"You know he's not much for crowds."

"He *saved* me!"

"I gathered."

"I should visit him before I leave."

"No, no. He's resting. But don't worry he's right where he ought to be. I stopped by his place on the way in and he was insistent that if I saw you to tell you something about something."

"What *is* it?"

The stranger looked up and to the left, as if trying to read lost bits of memory in the sky. Slowly, unsteadily he pulled something from his mind. "He knows I'm terrible with these sorts of things but he specifically insisted. The core...hold on...wait...the poor... the poor, the poor. No. The war...no...wait...if...the. Shoot. Ah. The-war-is o-ver. You can go home."

The broken words showered Pierre in numbness. He fell away, crept forward, and begged him to repeat. The second time, it came without pause. He couldn't believe it. He was going home.

"Thank you. Thank you, thank you. Thank—You have no—I can't—ahhhhhhh!"

The stranger smiled. "Mmm. My pleasure."

Chapter 42

Once she found out her nephew was going to the Great Excavation, she thought it'd be therapeutic. A gifted hiatus from all Caterwaul's expectations. She honestly hoped he'd find answers, get information, realize something to tide him over while he accepted this as his new home. The news from The Falklands never changed. Even before him, it was always some degree of turmoil, some tint of perilousness. That's why she left. Some cycles never end. She didn't expect history to up and change on its own, but she did her best to retain a naive optimism, for Pierre. To accept a place as home gives some power over the process. It makes you feel less out of place, grants an endowment of purpose, and an ability to claim. She wanted it so desperately for him. To gain resolution, and clarity, and wisdom but above all, contentment. But that's not how he returned. He ran through those mountains ecstatic. Wrangling her, the Sachem, and the crew of Catchers, and pushing them to the shore.

Aria stood in the staggered circle, with a stoned expression as Pierre told the story, in big animated gestures. Xander grinned, Cole blinked, the Sachem frowned, and Puddles just looked hungry, while Patricia spun questions. Aria asked how the Cape would compensate for his loss so quickly. Patricia wondered, with what he had to gain, did it matter? She wanted to know more about this suitor spreading the good word, but with Tiberius broken, what other sources did he have? This was his only information and her nephew was an adult now, officially with the passing of the mating season, entirely capable of his own discretion. She was a skeptic, but if he could go home, if even an ounce of that was true, what could she do? Her duty as an aunt was to show loving support.

As the Safety, however, she had another obligation. "Pierre, come here," she said, stepping on the less significant chatter, ushering him off to the side. She looked over her shoulder back at the group, most of them still arguing what was the proper emotional response, while Aria glanced nervously at her and Pierre.

"What is it?" Pierre said.

Patricia opened her beak for a long pause.

"I know you're excited but I can't let you leave." That came out wrong. She blinked. "I mean, you need to stay. We need you to stay. What I'm trying to say is, we need time?"

Pierre turned his head gazing out toward the dark sloshing waves over the moonlit sea. "How much?"

She scanned the floor, running the numbers in her mind. "Fourteen mornings."

Pierre's stern glare and clenched jaw were topped with a tensed brow. He softly shook his head. Patricia refused to acknowledge the motion. His hesitance made the air thick, and Patricia uncomfortably warm. She could feel herself creeping closer. Slanting. Imploring. "You don't owe us. But."

Pierre exhaled and walked down the shore. She took in a breath to say his name, but thought better of it. Standing where he was, she felt something plush bend beneath her feet. She stepped back. Two feathers lay between his large prints in the sand. Patricia hunched, brushed the pebbles, and moved herself out of the light. She saw what it was. Her eyes swelled and she was short of breath.

Chapter 43

Things were going better than planned. After Pierre's departure, Solus perused the worthless mound of junk hoarded at the Scavenger's Section, and spotted something of relative significance. He frowned and mumbled, stalking over to indulge the attendant, peeling off the droll enigmas, one by one, until the quota was reached. What was offered to him was a branch of some sort, supposedly special in healing. The vendor promised him with it came wholeness and rest. Solus scoffed. No branch could give him that. He waved it away as he bowed to examine something more fitting. An extension of his force, an embodiment of his might. Every ruler needed a scepter, every Poseidon a trident, and his pulse quickened while the crew fastened his prize.

A curious, abstract contraption salvaged from a more ancient part of the world where penguins were fought for blood sport. The item was loose, meant for a bigger foot than his. It drooped heavy when lifted. He stuck it out, admiring as it clanged in the wind, its partially rusted iron glinting in the dull light. Solus scraped his talons softly into the hard ice, making deep, crooked, effortless, grooves.

"Oh, yes," he scowled. "This will do."

Chapter 44

Hobbling down a long stretch on the southern tip of Africa, Tiberius worked around a bend and out of sight. Patricia smiled, thinking of his indomitable knack for exploration. It's what he'd been doing his whole life, and even in his throbbing, hurting condition, the large bird refused to be tied down. Now he got to view his home in a different way. While he was caged, Patricia made a point to keep him as the vault of her secrets. She never wanted his life to lack purpose. He was the only one she could talk to without feeling as though she were dropping a burden. Tiberius still listened, and she still talked. Enjoying his timely onomatopoeia and disapproving grunts during their sessions. They became very close. What are friendships but time and trust? Sharing the information, just to say it out loud, somehow went a long way to lighten the load. They had something that was theirs alone. A club, for members only and no one else.

The good news was that the doctors said in time, with continued care, his wounds would heal. But her biggest fear was that something would happen to her while he was injured and there would be no one able to deliver the news to her brother. To die in a paradise mourned by none of her own. The thought brought morose emotions, as old as her choice to leave home and find new land, was ultimately what led to the beginning of their partnership long ago. Amongst the fresh litter of Trans-Atlantic qualifiers, she attended she plucked him like fresh fruit from the last remaining lot of his peers. He was awkward, obtuse. A gangly frame that proved far too much to manage gracefully. It was hard watching him walk, and the other young albatross mocked his disproportions, snickering discreetly and sometimes not so discreetly at his crooked gait.

A shaky-legged newbie, Tiberius Flock couldn't plant half a dozen steps before tripping over his own appendages. Not helping were his long wings drug the ground, and thick heavy beak that tipped him forward while his large floppy feet slapped the sand like a walrus. Every reason not to pick him. Sure deformities on all accounts, but Patricia saw he was born special, forged for more of a specific calling. Following her heart, she believed in him when no one else did. Convinced, with proper nurturing, the objects of his ridicule could turn to the claim of his glory. As he came into his own, others who picked from that same lot grew embittered by the missed potential. Slyly trying to convince him to take on side-missions while he wasn't in use for Patricia. They offered more food, better housing, and less work. He never took them up on one of their solicitations. What Patricia and he developed over those years was sacred. They *chose* to care for one another, creating a bond that could only be accomplished through free will. She found an indescribable comfort in their covenant.

As Patricia stood, staring in a daze toward the place he once went, a citizen zigzagged toward her. The penguin moved as briskly as her body could manage. Patricia sighed. Penguins like Ethell were the bane of public service. Another sighting. Patricia geared up for her typical routine.

One. Inform: Solus has been Banished, and thus could not be here.

Two. Condescend: I doubt you saw what you think you saw. It's a common mistake.

Three. Console: But just to be sure I'll send someone to check on it, okay?

Since Banishment, Solus had become somewhat of a local boogeyman. An urban legend, like their very own phantom. Opportunistic parents used him as a tool, and fear tactic to drum obedience out of their fledglings. 'If you don't go to bed, the Banished will come get you.' Infatuated adolescents told tall tales of his crimes at night by the shore like some sort of macabre occult. Citizens, young and old, claimed glimpses of him in various places, yet each investigation revealed the culprit to be not much more than a shadow or rock. Her patience was waning.

The chances of Solus being alive right now were slim. The markings in his shoulders were universal symbols of the condemned. He would be able to access no other colonies. Bodies of the four previous exiles were all found by Messengers within seven days of dismissal. Opened, rotted, and dug into. What each of them failed to realize was in here they were sheltered. In here, they were looked out and provided for, granted protection and the benefit of institutions. The privileges of a good society so long as they did their parts, but out there, there was no such arrangement. Even the most malicious, the ones discovered of torture, constant violence, and murder quickly learned that the world was no place to be alone, and there was always something more dangerous than you.

The frantic penguin was close. "I saw him!" the frazzled elderly shouted, finally reaching Patricia. "Again!" She stood wide and leaned far back for air. "This time I'm sure! You have to send someone."

As the depository of fears, Patricia learned to approach her problems by probability. Evidence of Solus' existence or resurgence physically just wasn't there. Every hunt, every search did nothing more than remove valuable Preservers from their post. Throughout all the in-depth hunts not a trace had been found to support the claims. Why would he risk his life? Patricia wanted to ask, but refrained, knowing it would be snide. Out there, maybe he could outlast his predecessors, figure out something before something found him, but there was no hope in here. He would die instantly. Unfortunately, logic aside, every claim must be adequately looked into. Being responsible for Cape safety meant Patricia had to reserve room for being wrong.

She clouded annoyance with a vacant smile. "Okay, Ethell, I'll have someone check it out."

Ethell nodded, walking off muttering.

"Another one?" Ferdinand asked approaching with Pierre as they passed by Ethell.

"The more penguins *talk* about seeing him, the more they do."

Pierre leaned. "Who?"

His aunt and uncle consulted one another in a gaze.

"Solus," she answered.

"The Banishment your first day," Ferdinand added. "They think…he's back."

Chapter 45

Evil comes in many forms. Draped in fresh garb from the Garment District, Solus was flawlessly cloaked at the Great Excavation. The symbols and scars on his wings and chest were buried under deep layers of seaweed. Avoiding Cape natives was simple enough. Probably, because no one suspected his presence, assuming the nuisance had been eradicated by a natural order. Because of this, they came to Bouvet unaware. Unconscious of the threat that mingled between them. To others, his eyes were a cool and curious feature, a carnival trick, or a deathly illness. Some marveled, some looked apologetic, but with all the penguins of the known world present, he was hardly the only unique bird.

Currently perched atop a hill, Solus peered emptily on the commotion below. Now baring his marred body, Solus had stripped himself of the disguise. *It will do no good here.* Wiggling the trinket on his foot, Solus waited for his accomplice.

"I can't lie," the albatross said, out of breath from climbing the tall ascent, "I was very surprised to see Pierre walk back through those mountains. I thought the whole point of me sending him to the Great Excavation was so you could get rid of him."

"I did get rid of him," Solus said, not turning to greet his informant, "and your freedom is on the horizon."

"How can I be free, nothing has changed!"

Solus made a half-revolution. "It has. You thought I was going to kill him. That lacks clairvoyance. His death would be a distraction, an unwanted pull. Citizens would rally, strung together by their loss. They would mourn their beloved but no! We want them vacant. We want them ready to accept their true, neglected son returned to save the Cape in need. That is what we desire, adoration. Willful submission through appreciation. The strongest sense of obedience comes from gratitude. Something I'll have in abundance once I save them from starvation. Once I have mercy and spare their young. Once I prevent the second coming of The Lack. I will *be* their savior."

Tiberius lingered a few steps back from the Fiordland. "But he looks so normal. Better than normal actually, he's happier than I've ever seen."

"Good."

"If you didn't kill him, then what *did* you do to Pierre on that island?"

"I infected him with something that when used properly can be the most toxic substance there is. Hope. He thinks his family wants him. That they've sent for him, that the war is over, and his dreams have come true," Solus chuckled.

Tiberius searched the ground. "The war is worse than ever, you know that. I've told you that. Penguins are dying all over the place, he'd barely swim in alive."

Solus smiled. "Exactly. Let the foreign take care of the foreign. Leaving the minds here a blank slate, free to worship and soak in our regime."

"What if he survives?"

"If he does somehow manage to evade that death that is so thirstily waiting for him, he'd never leave his family in that condition. The moment he sees them is the moment he's left Caterwaul forever."

Tiberius paced back as he tucked his wings in tight.

Solus stepped toward him. "Ask yourself something. Why are you here?"

Tiberius frowned, rapping his beak. After a long pause he looked up. "Well, I suppose I was tired of not making my own decisions. Always under someone else's schedule. My entire life, measured in subservience. Getting to listen but never speak my own words. Deprived of a break or the option to fly for myself. I was concerned that when I died alone I'd have no memories of my own making. I suppose, I wanted to be free."

Solus grinned. "And did you ask for these things?"

"I suppose, I thought I shouldn't have to."

"Mmm," Solus mused. "To do what you want, when you want, without consequence. That's freedom. You yourself told me how Pierre dropped from doing one thing and picked up doing another. How freely he went to the Great Excavation when it wasn't even his turn. Could you so plainly do the same?"

Tiberius sighed, looking as if he doubted Patricia would grant him permission.

Solus nodded firmly. "You could never be free while he was here. You would've run errands 'til the day you died and then more after that. There needs to be a new order, a new way of seeing things. Trust me, I know. I was Banished for exercising freedom. So bury that remorse, albatross. You've made the best selection."

Footsteps came trudging up the sand. A face scrunched tracking the two very different prints in the sand.

"Hey! You're not supposed to be here!" A large Preserver rushed up the hill closing fast.

Solus lunged forward with the sharp attachments fitted to his claws and flushed them deep into the chest of the strong Emperor, plunging again and again until he was no more. The talons dripped with blood, sand sticking to the thick liquid. He sighed, bending his neck to the left.

"If he could find us so can the rest. I'll find another place until the time is right."

Brushing past the body, Solus left, with Tiberius not far behind.

Chapter 46

Starlight illuminated five white faces in the night. The Sachem cleared his throat. "When Solus was young, he would catch fish. Big fish. The biggest his beak could carry, and drag them back to the Cape. He would toss it ashore and…after a moment, slowly bend each of its fins until it popped and broke. He'd use his claws to cut off the tail and rake scales off its body. As the fish lay there, eyes bulging, mouth agape, deep gashes stretching along its side, Solus would step back and watch. Denying it release, instead just standing there, as if wanting to see how long it could live in pain, suffocating and hurt, squirming before it would submit. Before it would give in to exhaustion and the inevitable. Before it would welcome the end. He'd hunch over, whispering under his breath, "Maintenant tu sais comment je me sens…Now you know how I feel."

Pierre felt blood leave his face.

"After getting kicked out of the Builders sect," the Sachem continued, "he ended up here as a Catcher. His anger and rage were powerful fuels for a hunter and made Solus the best we'd ever known, before you. The Cape flourished in his harvest. Families reproduced rapidly, and, no one ever thought to worry."

Aria's gaze fell.

The Sachem peered over and sighed. "Until the disappearances. Mornings became half-days, half days became full, then days on end. Solus was nowhere to be found as crowds slept around the reserve waiting their fill. Production collapsed in every department as doctors and builders, teachers and guards could focus on little more than the famished quake rumbling inside of them. We tried to help. Working ourselves to the point of prostration, and every time we'd drag ourselves from the ocean, slightly disoriented, the crowd was so large we thought we were hallucinating. Seeing double. They lingered, famished with long gazes. That's when we saw it. He was the heart of our entire colony. We hunted exhaustively, but without his help we simply couldn't meet the need. There were too many. Citizens began to fight over who could eat first. Seniority, occupation, status, popularity, all of a sudden mattered. It was—"

"I took the responsibility," Patricia said, raising her head, "to protect them from threats inside and out. And this certainly fell in that category, but I didn't know how to protect them from this. Their questions turned to suggestions, before long, they were commands. Birds were shriveling in front of us and they wanted to know what I would do, demanding a solution to the death toll. What could I do, besides wait for it to balance out? Until the number of penguins matched the food. I saw this place becoming the Falklands. I'd never felt so helpless. I knew how to do all these things, but none of them could help me. We tried talking to Solus, bargaining for his aid. Explaining how his negligence was killing us. That we needed him, depended on him. But he was so pumped on his own hubris he didn't feel he had to listen to anybody. We had a part in that. The more I thought the more I wanted to know. Where was he going? What was so important, he'd risk our lives to get there? Well, one day, I had him followed. The Preservers tracked him far out in the ocean and deep into the lower abyss, where we lost the trail. They waited for Solus to resurface, but he never came up. According to the Wellness Ward, part of this story makes sense. In his last days, Solus was undergoing a process called bioluminescence, an adaptation for creatures of the deep. On the carcass of a fangtooth fish, we found gel in the eye sockets which fused to the visual cavity. The process seemed very painful, but once complete, we assumed the body's natural heat acted as an energy source. The bacteria would be endlessly lit so long as the body was alive. The end result, a luminous glow of the original eye color. Those who have undergone this evolution can see perfectly in the dark. When Solus finally returned to the Cape, we knew where he had been, but more importantly where he hadn't. Solus' Banishment was scheduled."

Pierre stiffened.

Aria's brow flexed so tight it trembled. "He was the reason for everything. I look back on my life and every significant moment, every meaningful decision was because of him. The Lack changed it all. I am his creation. As is Caterwaul. He taught us new fear, and we responded to it."

Chapter 47

Not long after the sober discussion, the fiery giant rose from his slumber. Pierre was waiting for him, as rays bled over the ocean. The day had arrived. An orange glow climbed from foot to face as Pierre couldn't help but think if he was making the right choice about Emily. He would still make the journey every Great Excavation but he knew leaving the Falklands would be much harder than walking out of Caterwaul. The dilemma tore at him as his dry eyes cringed in the sunrise. "Who needs you more?" he asked. "Who do you need more?" At this point he honestly wasn't sure. He wanted them both in his future and trying to prioritize was like paralleling opposites. They were his family, yet Emily made him so happy. Happier than he'd ever been. The recurrent, frothy waves offered no wisdom as birds above silently watched on.

For the Cape, the two weeks prepping for transition had gone as well as they could. Forcing the colony into impassioned think tanks for creative sustainable solutions. They pooled every resource, trying to restructure their division of labor to accommodate the food-supply system. The New Plan took advantage of the tireless crew of youth. Instead of delaying them with long training cycles, the Cape gave them opportunities to contribute to the catch earlier and more often. The Sachem outwardly objected to the program, saying he didn't like the danger it presented to future generations. But the way Patricia saw it, the need outweighed the risk. If they didn't catch, she said, they'd be dead anyway. Sheltering them was both impractical and impossible. Having to make up in numbers what they didn't have in experience or skill. Thus, the consensus was that some would be drafted into the profession, instead of choosing it of their own will. While everyone would be given an educational foundation, being required to serve in the hunt first before moving to their preferred role. Lastly, in a state of emergency, the order in which they would be drafted was agreed upon as follows: Builders, Instructors, Medical, Preservers, D.E.W.

With colliding, untested theories dampening the atmosphere there hung a nervous hush amongst the deciding parties. What if it didn't work? What if they were sending young hunters to die? What if outraged parents refused to send their youth into the water. How would the draft be enforced? By begging, by scaring, by might? Thoughts swam through Pierre's mind, knowing how fast partition can swell. He was concerned this choice might divide the colony. Nevertheless, this was it. The last day he could help. He had to trust they'd do their best, and remind himself that this place existed long before he did. His aunt already assured him, no matter how it turned out, she was with them. She wasn't running. Not again. This was her home, and this time she was going to fight for it.

From atop the hill, Pierre watched citizen traffic flow in one direction. The benediction was amongst him. A colony-wide reprieve had been taken from duty, as citizens were allowed to prepare for the commemoration. Pierre thought it much fuss, but his aunt was persistent. He rose, shaking the sand from his body, brushing the tiny pebbles pressed in dents in his flesh from the prolonged sitting. Pierre caught the assembly as Patricia trudged up the tanned ascension. Atop a small mound at the foot of the entrance, she called the pocketed clumps into order. As they consolidated, his aunt shot out a slight huff, before clearing her throat. "We are gathered here today to celebrate a very special contribution from one of our newest citizens. Though only here for a short a time, his impact will be felt for generations to come. And before you have a fun-filled day enjoying what we have now, I wanted to give our King the opportunity, to say a few words."

Pierre parted from the audience. Turning to face the crowd he lost his words. The population had grown to a massive metropolis, with penguins spread from mountain to sea, north to south, and from D.E.W. to the Academy, east to west. Standing on the platform where he once witnessed Banishment he addressed the crowd below:

"Um," he stuttered, "I have to go now."

"Speak up!" a voice cried in the back. "We can't hear you!"

"I have to go now." His deepened voice echoed and carried, delivering the painful fact like ripping a scab. "Leaving behind more than you know. When I came here, I only cared about what I was going through. What I had been through, but I learned, I'm not the only one with hardships. I am not the only one with pain. I didn't grow up here, young and curious like most of you but I did grow here. And that makes this more than a place. I've felt a responsibility to you, and a service, and that makes you more than citizens."

"Then why are you leaving?" another voice shouted from the crowd, full of anger, before being audibly shushed by those nearby. Pierre searched the mass for follow up. Maybe the penguin said what the others had too much decency to verbalize. His conscience panged. He grew warm. "You all are somebody's family, as, as am I. And I want to thank you for being so—"

"Don't leave us!"

"—Supportive. I understand change can be scary. Everything I'd known was shifted when I was sent to come here. Inside, I was confused, angry, and alone. But I've learned there is no growth without change. Me leaving will mean change for the both of us. And I hope you see your strength more than your hurt. Your purpose, more than your pain. I wish I could tell you challenges won't come. That wouldn't be true for you or me. What I can show you is what you've built. Through your will: builders, catchers, teachers, preservers, medics and D.E.Ws. I have confidence, not rooted in hope but in history. We've been here before, you and I. Shore torn from beneath our feet, and asked to survive. Knocked from out bliss in such a way we thought it was gone forever. But it has. We are restored. We are strong. We are not weak. We are not victims. We can protect our own joy. So nothing will *ever* take it again!"

The crowd paused, processing the words, then brayed with a loud voice lifting their beaks to the sky. The sound of slapping flippers ran through the colony.

Patricia moved up next to Pierre. "Go!" she said brimming, a twinkle in her eye. "Celebrate! Celebrate your families!"

The citizens spread in wide batches.

"You've grown up nephew."

Pierre looked at his aunt. Thankful of how she pushed the colony cheer a transition rather than grieve an exodus. Inspiring citizens to wield their destinies and build a better system relying on a diverse collection of resources, so no one penguin could ever break them down again.

Patricia leaned over, watching the innumerable splashes decorate the ocean. "Whether they know it or not, they *are* better off. We did this. We built this colony. And it is time we start acting like it." She smiled. "We've overcome so much, somewhere it was lost that our greatness isn't in the achievements but the ability to achieve."

Pierre nodded, feeling a little less heavy. As the gay stampede rushed into the breaking waves, a single body remained.

Chapter 48

"How dare you pick up and leave like this!" Sherri growled, the hot-blooded D.E.W stomping to his stoop.

"Sherri what're you talking about?" Pierre asked cautiously.

"This is abandon. This is neglect, this is an outrage, and you do it with a smile." She narrowed her gaze. "I won't celebrate this. There's no honor in what you're doing. No greatness, none at all."

"Sherri, what are you *talking* about?" Pierre asked, befuddled.

"You know exactly what I'm talking about! Look at you. Running off. Shirking your responsibility so you can go be young again. You know, I oughtta whoop yo—" she rushed up the hill.

"Sherri!" Patricia cut, stepping in, "it is his decision."

Sherri stopped and snarled like a hyena turned away by a lion. "If that's how much you care," she said, staring past the Safety, "then it is best you go." Sherri pounded to her cave, throwing looks of disgust over her shoulder.

"It's a good thing, Sherri!" Pierre shouted to her marching away.

"Good for who?" Her small voice carried from afar.

Pierre could only attribute the tirade to her concern for future generations. She was scared. It was all he could think of. Fearful of what him leaving could mean for the eggs. If he thought they were in ill-care…

Ferdinand walked up to Pierre's vacant side. "Sherri must've gotten a little sweet on you during your time together, ey." He hummed a laugh. "Ey."

Aria quietly joined the party.

"You can't expect everyone to be happy you're leaving." She giggled.

Wait a minute. He didn't know she could giggle. Besides the Great Excavation, the two of them spent every day together since he arrived. She checked his playful ego whenever it reached critical mass, and gave words of encouragement whenever he was sad about home.

Pierre was very grateful for her. She, more than anyone, made him feel a lot less alone. In the span between his announcement and departure, he noticed she was acting weird. Looking him in the eye more. Like she was now. Lingering after conversations, wanting to talk about more than work and the world that surrounds it. Her gaze, became less rigorous and concentrated, morphing to something threatening, bashful, glancing away whenever caught staring. It was very allusive.

"Are you sure you're ready?" Pierre turned to his aunt.

"Yes. We've held you long enough."

"You think I'm doing the right thing?"

Patricia looked him over, glancing at his stomach. "There are some situations, Pierre, where I can't tell you what to do. You're grown now and you have a tough choice. All I can say is, family first."

Pierre understood. This had to be his choice. Despite their kind imploring, he took nothing from the Reserve for his journey. Pierre said his goodbyes and trudged backward through the titanic mountains.

Far away, red eyes trailed the Catcher for several minutes until he was out of sight. With most everyone enjoying themselves far out to sea, it was time. Solus descended the seclusion and, on the heels of Pierre's farewell, entered the Cape.

Chapter 49

"Word around the Benguela is you're in need of a new Catcher?"

Patricia's body locked. A voice cold and chilling came from the shade between the mountains. She frowned. "Not like you." He was only a few feet away, but hopefully he would advance, giving her an opportunity to set diplomacy aside and lay him out cold.

Solus was in breach of his Banishment but she was no Preserver, and politics still called for an appropriate course of action. If the Fiordland wasn't threatening her life the most she could do was call the Preservers who have the authority to execute justice. As the matriarch of this community, one of the aggravating binds was she had to display restraint when it was not easy. If citizens could become executioner at their own private discretion, the Cape would quickly slip into a savage goop. Patricia grasped the importance of poise, but she burned with desire in its purest form to bludgeon until his bones cracked.

"You have no choice," Solus said with a smug twinge in a dry tone.

"Not many options, but there's always a choice. We're ready to take up the mantle."

He blurted, "The *Tee*-Waddlers? Who've never been on a real hunt in their lives? They're supposed to support this entire Colony?" He gestured in the dark spreading his flippers wide.

"Everyone's new at some point. What they lack in skill they'll make up for with persistence. They know what's at risk. We don't need you."

"Oh, Patricia," he uttered with a tut-tut, "how vain your optimism can be. With five rotations six times a day they still can't give the Cape what it needs. You know as well as I do that was a plan to pacify the dumb. A stall tactic to prevent real panic while you scraped together an answer. But solemnly, you already know the answer. Whether you like it or not I'm all you've got. The only legitimate course."

Patricia crumpled her brow. Detailed plans of what Caterwaul would do after Pierre was privy only to a few. How did he know?

Of course, she had her concerns of if the fresh, new Tees were ready. The magnitude of responsibility was unfair for a bird at any age but especially the young and untrained. The times required it, demanding they be more than they were, but she couldn't be sure they could answer the call. True, the Cape could use someone of Solus' capabilities. Until they got set. But not Solus. Clenching her jaw, she glared at him silently. She sensed the bulging muscles protruding from her face.

Solus spoke. "It's not about us or them. Or rules or customs or banishment. It is about survival. Rattling on the tremors of turmoil, will you make the correct decision or the right one?"

"Solus, we hate you."

"Ditto. There's no sense hiding true emotion, but that's not worth dying for. Those feelings will pass. Aided along by full bellies and happy families. The scar tissue between us will harden and the skin shall regain its color. In time it can be right, and that's exactly what I can give them, what I can give you. Time."

"Yours is a debt that cannot be repaid."

"Tell me, Patricia, O 'Safety of the Cape,' what will you say when the first of them start to go? Knowing you could've done something and did nothing, what will you tell the mothers and offspring, family and friends? What will you tell your albatross, your partner, yourself? That you did all you could? You did not. That you made the hard choices? This is the hard choice. Not everything can be solved with the combat you learned on the Falklands. It is your duty to protect them from threats inside and out?"

"That's what I'm doing."

"Not when you turn away what they require most. It's plain that I can help, but even more than me they need you. To be the guardian they can rely on. A leader that they can trust to make the best decision even if it's unpopular. Are your principles really worth more than yourselves, to die with your pride rather than live with compromise? Will you be small? Shrinking to the past, drowning in the quicksand of trespasses long ago? Or will you champion their future? Will you care? Will you save them? Will you rise? Am I worse than death? This might be your last chance."

Patricia paused in animation. Her gaze fell to the sand. Her muscles were still clenched, pulsing. Solus kept his space. Looking away, her posture dropped. Her eyes drooped. She cried, one tear after another until she collapsed into a trembling sob. The truth hurt so much she could hardly stand. *Why?*

"Before I give you my decision," she swallowed, "I have to know. When did he betray me? When did he tell you everything I told him?"

Buckled in the sand, her strong voice transformed to a quiver.

Solus approached cautiously, stepping from the dark. "When I started telling him everything you didn't. Truth is buoyant, Patricia. Even when you try to suppress it, eventually it will find a way to the surface. Your omissions kept him dormant, but beneath he was thirsting for deliverance. I gave him that, and loyalty, is always strongest toward the liberator."

Patricia wept. Water ran down the side of her face curling into her neck. She had known Tiberius his whole life. Loved him like the fledgling she was too barren to have. He listened when no one else would, keeping her secrets like the truest friend. What did he want to say? Why couldn't he tell her? Was he afraid? Grief, shock, depression, hurt clenched in the pit of her stomach, compounded by a searing guilt. She wasn't there for him the way he was for her.

Solus slid closer, talking softly, his shadow overlapping hers. "This is hard. It's terrible to be betrayed." Solus moved closer still as Patricia wept. "You've made some mistakes in the past. I can fix them. I'm here to help. All you have to do is let me."

His voice, now directly above her. She looked up blinking to clear the blur. "You're evil. Your father left you. Your mother hated you. I would have too. You're a worthless speck of scum and you deserve it. You deserve to have nothing. You deserve to be alone. You deserve to be Banished. And I won't give you our Cape to poison like you've done everything else. Nobody cares about you Solus, and no one ever will."

Patricia stared blankly, and then dropped back into a gentle sob. Solus could never have the Cape, for exactly the same reasons he wanted it. She just needed to know for sure. Solus took her only good friend.

Solus' glowing red eyes swelled as his body escalated in temperature. His chest pumped with hot air. He clenched his iron talons staring at the top of her head. He moved to the left, posturing. One hard thrust would impale this sharp metal through the side of her throat. He etched closer, his darkness slivering over her body. He steadied his breath, lifting to end her world. Before a slow blinking glint in the distance caught his sight. He lowered his claw, and left, leaving Patricia with her sorrow unaware.

Chapter 50

Pierre feared the other side of the island. Vacant monuments loomed as a painful reminder of the decision not made. His mortal shell, flocked, swarmed, haunted by warm palpitations whenever he'd recollect. He loved Emily. Their time together was real, but how do you choose?

His parents, ironically, had a similar start. With a rift of decisions between them, spinning innumerable possible outcomes. How did they choose? His dad didn't flee with Patricia, he chose not to take the chance when he could've gotten out. But was his life *better* for it? Why did he stay? Pierre wished he could talk to him now.

The troubled King walked the quiet white island, wrestling with the stubborn conundrum. His aunt's words hung in his mind: 'Family first.' But when everything was still, he only thought of Emily. Was *she* his family now?

A clearing ahead revealed a small structure as a blip that must've been Paul's home manifested in the distance. The break was welcomed. He crossed the traverse rushing up before he lost his footing on an oxford streak smeared messy and wide across the ice. The trail bent around the rubble as his gaze crawled up the path to the torn body of a mangled Fairy.

"Paul?" He stepped lightly not to wake him up. "Paul?"

Pierre tapped, he didn't move. He pushed Paul, and he rolled back limp. Pierre bent over the scarred body, baptizing it in droplets.

"It's okay. It's okay." Pierre lay next to his friend. His cheeks trembled, hot breath launching tiny clouds of smoke. Pierre's chest sunk on that grim grey island, and although he was taught adults weren't supposed to cry, he did it anyway. Who did this? He said he had no friends. Who else could've known where he lived? Pierre turned his neck, confused. Delio? Who was he? That bird from the Great Excavation. Pierre rose, asking the questions he should have asked at the festival. Where was he from? He knew his name. Pierre examined the crumbled structure. Turning north peering out toward Caterwaul. Delio Egnever. Delio Egnever. Delio Egnever.

Chapter 51

Booms of a drillship trembled the ocean. Solus pulled alongside the corroded hull as the bulging steel echoed an aggravated moan. Pressure was building ever since the Cape tried to remedy their little problem. This was Tiberius' greatest gift. The plugs were successful at stopping the toxin from flowing into the water, but with nowhere else to go, the dangerous substance pushed against every centimeter of the swollen frame.

Solus admired the chiseled fixtures. The ingenuity was an example of how aptly they could have served. Four pegs of talc were pushed deep into the hole. Solus pressed his ear to the ship, listening to it like a womb. Then he raised his sharp claw, kicking them loose, one by one. Sculpted pearlescent rocks ejected into the pure blue Atlantic and a surge of something shiny and black rushed into the sea.

The ill cargo seeped like tree roots as potent streams darkened the surroundings. The death he promised now took form. This was his triumph. Not the one intended, but the one they deserved. The cure for lack of compromise. He wanted to have the colony for himself, to lead to rule, to return the favor of pain and agony yes, but to also build his home anew. His clash with Patricia forced upon him an aggravating truth, one that dictators and bullies sooner or later all come to realize. There is no reasoning with idealists. He understood, now, how deeply burrowed their lack of love was for him. Offering a savior in their time of need, they would rather be wiped away than rescued by his embrace. So be it. He would purge their broken system and cleanse their stubborn pride with the quotient of their disobedience. They didn't deserve the land they held. This deluge would scrub Caterwaul so a new colony could start in its place. A proper society, a home made in his image. He would be appreciated. He would be loved.

The Cape was celebrating the farewell of their endeared King. Swimming in the ocean with their new families. Solus smiled. The poison was on its way.

Chapter 52

"I thought you were gone," Aria said very high pitched.

Xander, Colt, and Puddles spun around.

"I was. But—"

"Tentacles!" Ethell yelled, hobbling hurriedly toward the group. "Tentacles! Shiny tentacles. In the water!"

Aria frowned. "That doesn't make sense."

"It does," Pierre said "He released the poison."

"Who?" Colt asked.

The four looked down in shocked at Colt's square face and boxy figure boxy figure. This was the first time he ever spoke, and his voice was like a frog.

"Solus," Pierre responded.

Aria shook her head. "Solus is gone. Probably dead."

"He's not."

"How do you know?"

"I do."

"How!" she shouted.

The other members of the group bickered to the one standing next to them in debate.

"Because he told me. Right to my face what he was planning to do. Thought I'd never find out or not until it was too late. He introduced himself to me at the Great Excavation as Delio Egnever."

"So," she looked up. Blinked. "Oh, no." The revelation bleached her expression.

"He lured me away with a lie that my parents wanted me back. I didn't know who he was, but it didn't matter. I would've believed anyone."

"I'm sorry, Pierre." Aria's voice soft as petals.

The muscles in his jaw pressed his beak together. "The pollution in the water is from holes in the ocean skimmer."

"We plugged those," Xander said.

"Then they've been unplugged!" Pierre replied, standing over him.

"Why did you come back?" Aria asked. "Is that the only reason?"

"Where you want to be and where you need to can be two different things. Someone told me that. I should've listened."

Aria's flippers swung at her side.

"Right now we have to get everyone out of the water."

"How're we going to get them to shore?" Puddles asked.

"The ones that are well enough will latch on to our back and we'll swim them in. Just like Resistance Drills."

Colt departed quickly.

Pierre turned to Puddles. "Tell Sachem, and rally every Catcher in the academy that isn't out to sea. This is the most important haul of their lives."

Puddles nodded and made haste.

Pierre turned to Xander. "I need you to tell the albatross, Pickers, Couriers, and Messengers to fly over and scan. When they see stranded birds in the water, circle above so we'll know their location. Underwater visibility won't be great. We'll need markers in the sky."

"Or the albatross could do the work for us and we can stay here," Xander responded.

"No, we're too heavy, and we'd sink them. This is no time to argue. It has to be us. Avoid the contaminant at all costs. The darker the water the bigger the danger. The faster this happens the better. Remember, he's here so *be careful*."

As Pierre turned toward the sea, a three-letter word drifted into his ear. "Dad?"

Chapter 53

A shower tingled crown to foot as a little reflection stood so small nearly a fourth of his body was covered in sand. His face was cheeks, and everything else worked around them. Eyes shimmered flecks of chocolate and emerald. Pierre moved to the loose bowtie around his neck. Emily.

"Congratulations," Aria whispered weakly.

Pierre stumbled forward. The shedding of feathers wasn't his annual molt. It was the beginning of a brood patch. That night atop the trails. If he had only known.

"It's me," Pierre said smiling.

The youth stirred with one foot and puts his chin in his chest.

"Pierre!" Emily ran up, pressing her face against Pierre's.

Aria glowered. "Pierre, we have to go," she snapped with an iron diction. "The team and I are leaving. We hope to see you out there." Aria trailed Emily up and down narrowing her eyes. Then walked away.

Emily frowned and shifted to her mate. "I was only a few steps behind when he took off running. He's so low to the ground, wait, what's all this commotion. What is going on?" She swung her beak in a panoramic.

"Poison," Pierre said calmly, bending down. "In the water. And what's your name?"

"Tim," replied a small voice.

Pierre smirked at Emily. "That's my daddy's name. Are you my dad?"

Tim laughed.

Emily touched Tim at his shoulders. "I figured this could give you a bit of home."

Water rushed to his ducts.

"What are you going to do about the poison?" she asked.

"Citizens. At sea. We have to save them." Pierre spoke, never looking up.

"You're going in?"

"Have to. They need us."

"Umm!" Emily motioned from her to Timmy.

"I can't be selfish."

"You can."

"I won't." He rose.

She leaned forward. "Listen. You are not going to leave me. I just watched my mom die. Tim won't do the same with you." The words rushed out hot and hushed. She glanced down at Tim. "This is *their* Cape, Pierre. Theirs. Not yours. You've given enough. Come on now," she begged. "We need you."

Pierre gazed at his son, scooped under her wing. "Emily I'm sorry. I..." She shook her head and pulled away. "Somebody else will feel just like this very soon too if I don't go help right now. If I can save them, you would want me to, right?"

She looked him in the eye, "I'm not sure."

"That cannot be an option. I love you." Pierre stooped, shifting focus. "I'll make a promise to you. I'm coming back. I'm going to spend the rest of my life with you. I'm going to be your father."

Emily jittered, nodding. "I understand, but I don't care. I want to have something, something good, without it being taken away."

"I'm coming back for you," Pierre whispered in her ear. He then covered them in a long embrace and nestled his head against theirs.

Patricia rushed up. She glanced from Pierre to Emily to Timmy. "Come with me," she said to Emily, "we could use your help with the ones on shore."

Patricia pressed Emily down the sand with Tim alongside. She looked back over her shoulder with a smile.

Chapter 54

"Pierre!" Aria yelled trudging out of the sea, dumping a heavy black-footed penguin to the ground. "It's gotten thicker!" She gasped and dove back in.

The small lot who made it back on their own were gagging and wheezing by the lapping surf. Catchers were already dropping off the first survivors dripping with slime.

Pierre followed her to the break of the ocean when something dark caught his peripheral. He glanced over to an unforgettable face, poised, standing beyond the commotion. Pierre burst in his direction, ruffling through the growing, swarming mischief. The ominous callous figure stared back as if they were the only ones there.

"Murderer," Pierre growled.

"Thief," Solus returned. "But what's in a name? We are who we think we are."

Pierre moved closer. Tiberius slid back, trying to shrink behind a tall rock.

"Liar!" Pierre shouted.

Solus laughed, "They didn't send you away because the war was getting better, they sent you away because it was getting worse. Which means, in actuality, your parents are probably dead."

Pierre clenched to a knot.

"Welcome to the family. Oh! But, I can't take all the credit. I had help from a friend."

Tiberius fell, trying to move from one spot to another, and made a loud puff in the sand. Pierre burned through him with eyes like African fire. Tiberius kicked himself back into one of the domes until his body was in the dark.

Solus never removed his gaze from the King. The corners of his mouth rose and sank thinly, attempting to compose himself.

Pierre stepped toward Tiberius. The bird betrayed everyone. He stepped again. He helped Solus. He stepped again. He gave Solus information about the oil. Pierre took another step, and Paul's mangled body flashed in his mind. He turned.

"He's not my friend," Pierre said, scowling into the shadows. "You *killed* my friend."

Solus arched his eyebrows. Then shrugged.

"Well, you won't kill anyone else." Pierre stepped close, flaunting the slight height advantage in his favor.

Solus lowered his neck. "But there's only one left," he grumbled, lifting an iron claw, hidden under the sand.

Chapter 55

Patricia and Emily hustled down the shore with Tim in tow. An open plantation of oiled penguins lay moaning in the sand as they came to a stop. The few functional medics enough bounced back and forth between ailing patients. The instantly primitive medicines did nothing for the heightened sickness. Wraps and aquatic plants weren't working, and the despondent doctors wore the reality openly. They spent their lives dedicated to wellness, to the repair of the penguin body, but in the moment they were needed most, they felt helpless as any other.

The sound of a loud dry cough shot a shudder through Emily. Patricia didn't waste time. She knew what it looked like. When there was nothing left to do but comfort. She pointed Emily to a body and sat in the sand to the one at her feet. Emily lowered, talking gently to an elderly Gentoo. Her feathers had started to shed exposing spots of bare skin on her neck and face. She searched beyond Emily as her eyes focused, just realizing how close she was.

Patricia glanced over, stroking the head of a regurgitating Adelie.

She heard Emily talk to the victim.

"The world is better off for having had you. You're loved, and what you leave will keep you in warm memory." Emily smiled as the bird went dim. She looked up at Patricia, then over her shoulder. She frowned.

"Patricia, have you seen Tim?"

Patricia peered past Emily to a small pit where he was standing, and shook her head gently. Emily looked back down at the Gentoo, who had settled for sleep. Rising to for a full view, Emily cawed, loud as she could, and listened for a response. Patricia stood, calling for Pierre.

Emily's breaths were loud. "I've got to find him."

Patricia nodded firmly. "Let's go."

They took off. Sloshing down the shore, Patricia halted Emily with a flipper as something colossal threatened to trample them both. Their beaks loosened as the giant form stalked past. Patricia looked up. There were dozens of them. Hairless tree dwellers abducting citizens and planting them in vessels. Thirteen transports plucked citizens from the thinning Cape, looking to swoop the sick and wounded first. Most of those who remained cowered and fled from the giant titans, while some stood erect, wings wide, wanting to be taken. The two ducked outstretched arms weaving boat to boat. Dark brown canoes were rammed low into the sand, allowing Emily to barely hop up and see inside the wooden transports.

Stretching her neck, she got flashes inside of flustered victims. Shaking, yelling, and huddled in bunches. Birds, stripped of their natural color.

A loud dragging sound ripped their focus as the slush on the far side was followed by departure. A canoe dislodged limply and paddled away.

The Cape shriveled to less than twenty, dwindling to two types, the dead and gone. Patricia and Emily spun around. Did he try to follow Pierre? Two more boats slunk off, moving fast.

"Keep looking!"

Scurrying, the mother was systemic. Jump, look, call. Jump. Look. Call. Patricia saw her jump higher than before on each effort. Three boats remained. While they checked seven, nine took off. Emily leapt higher, more desperate, off-balance as a boat rocked off the shore, butting her in the stomach and toppling her into the crowded vessel.

"Emily!" Patricia shouted. "Emily!"

Chapter 56

Solus lunged. A beak hissed by both sides of Pierre's throat. He dodged them thinly, swerving left to right. Pellets of sand rained from Solus' metal claws as he pulled them from undercover. Pierre jumped back as the blades reach full extension and are forced to recoil. Momentum carried Pierre into a backpedal as Solus charged. Pierre stuck a stance.

Sidestepping, the King leveled a thick flipper on the Fiordland's vertebrae. A gust of wind sprung from Solus' body and Pierre followed with a blow for the head. Solus ducked under the limb, tripping forward and head-butting Pierre in the chest. Pierre spun in tattered revolutions before locking to a stop, batting two wild swings. Solus stepped up into open space and plunged a trident of claws into Pierre's gut.

Pierre howled and hunched. Solus pushed, driving them deeper. Blood from the punctured flesh oozed around the talons. Pierre yelled clapping hard on both sides of Solus' head. The Fiordland crumbled in a splash. Wincing, Pierre moved unsteadily. Solus crawled away, staggered, then stood, stumbled, stood up, and stumbled again. His red eyes shrank to a squint.

Pierre closed the land between them. Now at the base of his body, Solus flipped over fast and struck him with a kick. Something snapped in Pierre's left leg as Solus dragged himself to sea. Pierre buckled over then gimped in pursuit. Tripping into the ocean, the hard slap of salty water bit at his open wound. The tide waved him back, then pulled him in. Below, the stained water took a dim steel hue with sudden pockets of pitch caused by the varying thickness of contamination.

Bubbling through a light grey haze, fiery circles stared back in his direction. Pierre scrunched his neck and picked up speed. He'd seen what Solus was. Pierre knew penguins like him back home. Saw what they grew to become. If left alive, more were sure to die. Someway. Somewhere. Somehow. It was the motor of their soul. Banishment was just the latest excuse to justify harm, but no matter the front or feigned cause Solus was a well of mortality. One that had to be tapped. This would not become the Falklands. He would not watch his son grow up in the same way he did. This must be stopped. Now.

Pierre blazed deeper. The blue ocean stretched like a leopard with poisonous black spots three and four body lengths long. Each time he riffled through one, the gap narrowed. Erratic glimpses shot back through the murky aquatic. Pierre churned closer. So near he could feel the drift coming from Solus' tail. Stretching to snatch his prey, Pierre entered a nebulous pocket and never came out.

Pierre stopped, listened. They were close to the source. A foreign moaning of metal cloaked the enemy's slither. Pierre knew just because he didn't see him, didn't mean he was gone. Solus fled here for an advantage. Because it felt like home. Releasing the darkness of the ship, Solus raised the deep. Creating a pit similar to where Solus probably gained his bioluminescence. An ability he was sure Solus was using right now while he couldn't see a thing.

Pierre was stranger to this place. This void, this chasm. Even in the darkest of times, he was surrounded by bright things. Pierre shook his head as the toxin seeped through his shut beak. The oil on his tongue was pungent and sharp. He blinked hard as it touched his eyes. The substance burned as it entered his open wounds. Pierre tried to concentrate. He'd need oxygen soon. Alone, with the dangerous, only his thumping heartbeat resonated. The signature red light was nowhere to be found. Pierre rotated slowly. A flash of light split the dark. He parried, causing a near miss.

He narrowed his vision trying to see where Solus bolted off, but the stinging substance forced them shut to protect themselves from the toxin. Pierre hovered, blind and upright. A tingling sound arced around him. Iron claws rubbed together, moving independently as the flow of the water rushed between them. The sound was coming fast. Pierre saw a close light through his eyelids. He opened. Solus turned his back to Pierre, and drug the pointed metal across the width his chest. Pierre shouted, a cluster of bubbles searching for the surface. The iron, jingling again. Pierre leaned, dodging the swipe for his neck and bit hard on the high part of Solus' outstretched leg. The Fiordland towed him as he clenched stubbornly to the bone. Crashing through the surface, Solus cracked down hard on the penguin clamped to his foot. One! Two! Three! Pierre was jarred loose, his body awkwardly limp. The contraption hit the water alone, and then sunk, rattling into oblivion. The blunt force knocked Pierre into a fuzzy limbo. He heard voices. Flashes of dark colors that pulsated and glowed. Silhouettes, talking in the fog.

"All I can say is family first."

"Dad?"

"You've got a lot to live for now."

"I promise."

"I need you."

"I promise."

The noise marched closer, the sounds repeating themselves in succession. Louder. Closer. Louder. Closer. Until they were jumbled, screaming in his face. Pierre came to, Solus just a breath away, inspecting him. Pierre latched to his throat. Solus, twirled, swung, and slapped trying to pry him off as he swam like a wild balloon losing air. The blows shot pain through Pierre's skull. Patricia. Ferdinand. Solus pushed his face. Aria. Paul. Solus dug his beak into Pierre's shoulder. Emily. Timmy. Pierre squeezed so tight his jaw clicked. Pierre felt a shock go through Solus, as his struggle became less forceful, patting Pierre for mercy. Pierre suffocated the monster until he could feel no more life, and then held on longer.

Finding the closure, Pierre released him into the ocean and that horrid red glow went cold as it drained from Solus' eyes. The dark contamination moved like Death to claim that part of the sea and Solus was swept inside of a black cloud.

Chapter 57

After Emily vanished into the boat, Patricia was nabbed and dropped firmly into a half-wooden shell herself. The birds were hysterical. A tall Galapagos struggled to get over the ledge as a nearby party fought to keep her in, being pushed to and fro by her mad strength. She wailed, and snapped, yelling at the sea. Patricia witnessed the cause of her despair. Hoards, still as settled snow, bobbed on the ocean. They pushed past, their boat parting the graveyard. Patricia couldn't watch. Was ignorance better than panic? She wanted to protect them. She wanted them to have peace, but in the end they never had a choice. Patricia dropped from her tiptoes and walked the length of the transport wincing from how rough the hairless tree-dweller had handled her. She absorbed expressions of each shattered refugee. She kept this from them. She let this happen. She wasn't a protector. Even Tiberius abandoned her. Where was her mate? Where was her brother's son? She left Death in the Falklands, but it found her again, as she learned it always would. It had taken everything. With nothing left to start fresh with. She lifted her head as sun reflected off her watery eyes. Sighed. Tiberius. This was too much to bear. It was time to let go. saw the oil, She hopped up on the ledge, took a breath, and tipped herself in.

Chapter 58

Twelve canoes pulled toward the falling sun. The only things moving in the sea. Pierre glanced at the completely bare shore and bolted behind them. The effects of the poison started to mount as his adrenaline waned. Blurry pictures of birds huddled in crèches rose and fell and Pierre porpoised to glance inside the carriers. Where was the bowtie? He flopped back into the ocean, thrusting. He hopped alongside two more boats. His strength was drying up, now barely able to clear above the side. He had taken in too much. His heart pumped a thick, slow rhythm. Straining for elevation, his body drifted, locking mid-flight, crashing him into the sloped inner wall of a crowded vessel.

Pierre convulsed, clenching, oil dripped from the side of his face. Something blurry and large stomped toward him, pounding the wood and blocking the light. It split his beak and pushed what felt like a small round eel down his throat. He gaged. Cold liquid poured into his gut. He started swinging his flippers until they were pinned and a sharp stick plunged into his midsection. The small round eel was pulled from his throat. He gasped as it let up on his flippers and he rolled to the side. Pierre blinked, frowning as a strong force flipped him over. A spike pierced the nerves in his back. He shouted, twisting his torso, but he was pinned to the sand-sprinkled floor. Warm blood spread from the spot of the prick, coursing around his ribs, heating his heart. Black gunk trickled from the corner of his beak into a slow-moving pool spreading away from him. Pierre lifted his head. It was pushed back down, his cheek mushed against the wood. He grunted, beat his flippers against his side. His eyelids drooped to half-mass.

The swell in his stomach deflated as he was gently rolled over. Pierre relaxed to a trembling Gentoo arresting him with a hard hug as a small Tim resting his head on the spot below Pierre's wounds. Pierre sighed and rested his head back on the wood. The Cape was gone. They had no clue where they were going. For now, they had each other, and that was enough.

Chapter 59

The violence outside succumbed to a steady hush. Tiberius hid in a vacant home, wanting nothing more than to dodge his due portion. Solus had gorged him with delusional affirmations, painting him as brave, upright, and doing what must be done. But Tiberius learned a decision after the fact is less what you think of it and more what you feel. In his sobering moments, he didn't feel brave. He didn't feel upright. His alliance had him cowering in a dome, hoping never to see anyone who trusted him. Mostly, hoping never to see his friends. And right now, that was what he knew them to be.

Tiberius peaked outside, ducked back, then poked out his head once more. His pupils constricted to an open, vacant home as he stepped from the dark. His eyes sprung large. He sloshed the length of the shore, shouting. He yelled into the cave, then the academy, and every home between. Echoes. He stopped, bellowed once more, and collapsed. There were no Catchers bring him food. No Preservers to protect him from the things of the forest. And no medics to help him recover. He lifted a bent wing and pain shot through half of his body. He stood whimpering as it hung heavy and crooked. He turned to the forest, then the ocean. Trapped between equally dangerous habitats with fanged ravenous predators scouring, preying on the wounded, Tiberius slumped. Destined to wilt, until nothing was left but loose skin, and brittle bone.

Epilogue

Navigating the field of bobbing corpses, a rescuer rounded back for grim hope of survivors. Ossified bodies bumped like thick logs against the hollow canoe. A vision unsettling to anyone who cared about the value of life. Not because it happened, seabirds die every day like people do, but because it didn't have to. As the field of penguins scarred the top of the tainted Atlantic, the only two sounds were slow rolls of the evening waves and the gentle clatter of an iron lantern hung from a pole in front the ship. Minutes turned on the desolate landscape as darkness approached.

Standing to search far as he could one last time, the rescuer caught a subtle twitch in the far water. He steadied, knowing the oscillating sea could create illusions of movement. Seconds passed and the twitch shook again, then every few moments as if on a timer. Mark pointed the canoe to that section and slowly sifted through gaps in carcasses. Arriving, he raised his oars, plucking the bird from the thick slime and laying the creature on his lap. He parted the beak and worked a medicated fish down into the bird's throat before its subconscious reflex swallows the portion. The first signs of life. The worker was relieved but many dangers remained that could cause swift demise. He wasn't in the clear. Mark skipped the proper procedural order going straight for the mini-defibrillator he borrowed without permission. He was warned, using this at the wrong time could fry the heart. But his personal theories claimed otherwise. Clicking it on, he charged the grips rubbing them together. Its body gave a loud pop as he shocked the penguin once. Its chest adhered to the metal arching its spine.

After the climbing ting, the instrument was ready for round two. He administered the charge with a deep choom as different muscles quivered and tightened. A rattle of the flipper, a shake of the foot, a roll of the torso, then stiff rigor before relaxing into a disturbing stillness. The rescuer gritted his teeth looking away, dead bird in lap. Tears muddled his sight as purples, oranges, whites, blues, and golds raced across the South African sky. The rescuer sat there, in the newness of silent twilight with the numbness of what just happened. As the sun ebbed from the canoe, his lantern on a pole hummed to life. The rhythmic metal fixture gently rapped the poles in response to the waves.

Mustering courage to replace the still cadaver for collections in the morn, he gazed down to a set of quiet, open eyes watching him. They were calm, as if they'd been staring the whole time, with breath so subtle it could neither be felt nor heard. Mark brushed under his smooth chin with the back of his wrist, collecting the wetness before clearing some hardened ooze from the bird's cheek. The rescuer smiled a smile without teeth. The patient shivered as a cold air penetrated its vulnerable coat. Mark jiggled something out of a plastic box, and slipped the small emergency insulated cover over its chest and flippers to avert hypothermia.

Setting the bird down and gingerly stepping back over to the oars, the ferryman moved them through the graveyard. His sense of pride was inescapable. Mark had dared to double back when others said there was no point, and saved a creature, hanging by a thread. In his crowning glory, he smirked, thinking how he must've rescued the most unique penguin in the world. A brow, yellow as lightning and eyes like the faint spark of fire.

OISEAU THE KING CATCHER

In loving memory of Shirley Brown